SULPHURIC ACID

Belgian by nationality, Amélie Nothomb was born in Kobe, Japan, and currently lives in Paris. Described in the *New York Times* as 'slyly outrageous' and by the *Financial Times* as 'a charming little monster' she is the bestselling author of fifteen novels, translated into thirty languages. Her UK debut, *The Book of Proper Names*, was published to considerable acclaim in 2004.

AMÉLIE NOTHOMB
Sulphuric Acid

Translated from the French
by Shaun Whiteside

faber and faber

First published under the title *Acide Sulfurique*
© Editions Albin Michel S.A. – Paris, 2005

First published in the UK in 2007
by Faber and Faber Limited
3 Queen Square London WC1N 3AU
This paperback edition published in 2008

Typeset by Faber and Faber Limited
Printed in England by CPI Bookmarque, Croydon

A CIP record for this book
is available from the British Library

ISBN 978–0571–23493–6

2 4 6 8 10 9 7 5 3 1

SULPHURIC ACID

Part One

The time came when the suffering of others was not enough for them; they needed the spectacle of it, too.

No skill was required to be arrested. The raids occurred all over the place: anyone and everyone could be taken away, with no chance of dispensation. Being human was the sole criterion.

That morning, Pannonique had gone out for a walk in the Jardin des Plantes. The organisers came and scoured the park. Pannonique ended up in a lorry.

That was before the first broadcast: people didn't yet know what was going to happen to them. They were furious. At the station, they were piled into a cattle-truck. Pannonique saw that they were being filmed: several cameras escorted them, missing not a crumb of their anxiety.

It was then that she understood not only that revolt would be pointless, it would also be telegenic. So she became a marble statue for the whole of the long journey. All around her children were crying, adults grumbling, old people suffocating.

They were let out into a camp like the ones, still not very old, used for the Nazi deportations, apart from one notable exception: there were surveillance cameras installed everywhere.

No skill was required to be a guard. The bosses had the candidates parade in front of them, and kept the ones with the 'most meaningful faces'. Then they had to fill in questionnaires about their behaviour.

Zdena passed, and she had never passed an exam in her life. She was extremely proud of the fact. Henceforth, she could tell people that she worked in television. At the age of twenty, without a qualification to her name, she had her first job: her mates would finally stop making fun of her.

The principles of the programme were explained to her. The organisers asked her if she was shocked.

'No. It's brilliant,' she replied.

The headhunter thoughtfully said that that was exactly what it was.

'It's what people want,' he added. 'Soppy affectations are a thing of the past.'

She passed other tests, in which she proved that she was capable of beating strangers, of shouting gratuitous insults, imposing her authority, being left unmoved by entreaties.

'What matters is the respect of the audience,' said one of the organisers. 'No viewer deserves our contempt.'

Zdena agreed.

She was given the post of kapo.

'We'll call you Kapo Zdena,' she was told.

She liked the military term.

'You've got balls, Kapo Zdena,' she said to her reflection in the mirror.

She'd already stopped noticing that she was being filmed.

It was the only thing the papers could talk about. Editorials raged, solemn pundits thundered.

The public roared for more, from the very first broadcast. The programme, called simply *Concentration*, won record viewing figures. Never had people had such live access to horror.

'Something's happening,' people said.

The camera had something to film. It trained its many eyes on the huts in which the prisoners were penned: latrines, effectively, with straw mattresses on bunks, one above the other. The commentator spoke of the smell of urine and the damp cold which television, alas, could not convey.

The kapos were allowed several minutes to introduce themselves.

Zdena couldn't get over it. The camera would have eyes for her alone for over five hundred seconds. And that synthetic eye meant millions of fleshly ones.

'Don't waste that opportunity to make people like you,' one of the organisers told the kapos. 'The audience sees you as thick-skinned brutes; show them you're human.'

'And don't forget that television can also serve as a soap-box for those of you who have ideas, or ideals,' whispered another, with a perverse smile that said a lot about the atrocities he hoped to hear them come up with.

Zdena wondered if she had any ideas. The hubbub that she had in her head, and which she pompously called her thoughts, did not so deafen her that she could conclude in the affirmative. But she considered that she would have no difficulty in winning people over.

It's a common form of naivety: people don't know how ugly television makes them. Zdena practised her long-winded speech in front of the mirror, unaware that the camera would not treat her as indulgently as her reflection did.

The viewers couldn't wait for the sequences involving the kapos: they knew that they might hate them, and that they would deserve that hatred, indeed that the kapos themselves would supply additional arguments for their own execration.

And the spectators were not disappointed. In terms of abject mediocrity, the declarations of the kapos exceeded their wildest dreams.

They were particularly revolted by a young woman with a rough-hewn face, by the name of Zdena.

'I'm twenty years old, I'm trying to accumulate experiences,' she said. 'You should come to *Concentration* with an open mind. And besides, I think you should never judge, because who are we to judge? When I've finished shooting, in a year's time, there'll be some point to thinking about it. But not now. I know some people say that what we're doing to people here isn't normal. So to them I put this question: What's normality? What are good and evil? It's all cultural.'

'But Kapo Zdena,' the organiser butted in, 'would you like to be treated as these prisoners are being treated?'

'That's a dishonest question. First of all, we don't know what the inmates think, because the organisers don't ask them. It's quite possible that they don't think anything at all.'

'When you cut open a living fish, it doesn't cry out. Do you conclude from that, Kapo Zdena, that it does not suffer?'

'That's a good one, I'll remember that,' she said with a loud laugh that was supposed to be winning. 'You know what, I think that if they're in prison there must be a reason for it. Say what you like, I don't think it's a matter of chance that it's the weak who end up in here. What I've worked out is that I'm not a softy, I'm on the side of the strong. I was like that even at school. In the playground, there were the little girls and the sissies: I never joined them, I was with the hard guys. I never wanted to be moved to pity.'

'Do you think that the prisoners try to attract pity?'

'Of course, they cast themselves in a good light.'

'Very good, Kapo Zdena. Thank you for your honesty.'

The girl left the range of the camera, dazzled by what she had said. She didn't know she had so many thoughts in her head. She was delighted by the excellent impression that she thought she had given of herself.

The newspapers were filled with diatribes about the nihilistic cynicism of the kapos and in particular of Kapo Zdena, whose ideas of teaching people lessons caused a certain amount of consternation. The editorial writers returned frequently to this pearl, the idea that the prisoners were cast in a good light: the letters page spoke of smug stupidity and the poverty of the human spirit.

Zdena was at a loss to understand the flood of contempt to which she was exposed. Not for a moment did she think that she had expressed herself badly. She concluded simply that viewers and journalists were snobs, sneering at her for her lack of education; she put their reactions down to their hatred of the lumpenproletariat. 'And to think that I respect them!' she said to herself.

Moreover, she quickly stopped respecting them. Her

esteem was reserved entirely for the organisers, to the exclusion of the rest of the world. 'At least they don't judge me. The proof is that they pay me. And they pay me well.' One mistake per sentence: the bosses despised Zdena. They were taking her for a ride. And paying her badly.

Conversely, if there had been the slightest possibility of one or other of the prisoners leaving the camp, which was not the case, he would have been welcomed as a hero. The public admired the victims. The programme's great skill lay in presenting the most worthy image of them.

The prisoners didn't know which of them were being filmed, or which the viewers saw. That was part of their torture. Those who cracked were terribly afraid of being telegenic: along with the pain of their torment there was the shame of becoming an attraction. And the camera did not scorn the moments of hysteria.

Nor did it favour them. It knew that it was in the interests of *Concentration* to display to the maximum the beauty of that tormented humanity. So it was that it quickly chose Pannonique.

Pannonique had no knowledge of this. And that was what saved her. Had she suspected that she was the camera's favourite target, she could never have endured it. But she was convinced that such a sadistic programme was interested solely in suffering.

So she set about showing no pain.

Each morning, when the selectors were inspecting the inmates to decree which of them had become incapable of work and would be sent to their deaths, Pannonique concealed her anxiety and disgust behind a mask of superiority.

Then, when she spent the day clearing away the debris from the pointless tunnel that the prisoners were being forced to dig beneath the blows of the kapos' cudgels, she did not turn a hair. Finally, when these starving people were served their filthy soup in the evening, she swallowed it down without a flicker. Pannonique was twenty, and had the most sublime face imaginable. Before the raid, she had been a student of palaeontology. Her passion for the diplodocus had not left her with much time to look at herself in mirrors, or to devote her radiant youth to love. Her intelligence made her splendour yet more terrifying.

The organisers soon started showing her over and over, and seeing her, quite rightly, as one of *Concentration*'s major assets. That so beautiful and graceful a girl should have been destined for a death that would be witnessed live created an unbearable and irresistible tension.

In the meantime, the public could not be deprived of the delectations promised by such a beautiful girl: blows rained down on her ravishing body, not too hard, so as not to damage it too much, but enough to provoke the purest horror. The kapos were also allowed to throw insults, and showed no compunction in insulting Pannonique most vilely, prompting an intense emotional reaction in the viewing public.

The first time Zdena spotted Pannonique, she pulled a face.

There was something there that she'd never seen before. What was it? She'd met loads of people in her life, but never before had she seen whatever it was that she saw on this girl's face. And she didn't know if it was on her face, or in it.

Perhaps both, she said to herself with a mixture of fear and revulsion. Zdena hated this thing that made her so uneasy. It clutched her heart as if she'd just eaten something indigestible.

Kapo Zdena thought about it again during the night. She gradually became aware that she was thinking about it all the time. If she'd been asked what *it* was, she couldn't have given an answer.

During the day, she arranged things so that she could be in Pannonique's company as frequently as possible, to watch her on the sly and work out why she was so obsessed by the girl's appearance.

And yet the more she studied her, the less she understood. She had a very vague memory of the history lessons she'd had at school when she was about twelve. Her textbook contained reproductions of paintings by the old masters – she would have had trouble telling whether they were from the Middle Ages or some later century. They sometimes showed ladies – maidens? princesses? – who had that same mystery on and in their faces.

As a teenager, she had thought she was imagining it. Faces like that didn't exist. She had been able to confirm that in her own immediate circle. It couldn't be physical beauty, the girls on television who were supposed to be beautiful weren't like that.

And now she saw it on a stranger's face. So it did exist, after all. What was it that made you so ill at ease when you saw it? Why did you want to start crying? Was she the only one who felt like that?

Zdena lost sleep. Swellings formed under her eyes. The magazines declared that the stupidest of the kapos was starting to look more and more like a brute.

From the moment of their arrival in the camp, the prisoners had been stripped of their clothes, and had received a regulation uniform – pyjamas for the men, an overall for the women. A service number tattooed into their skin became their only permitted form of identification.

CKZ 114 – that was what Pannonique was called – was by now the viewers' muse. The newspapers devoted articles to this admirable young woman, the epitome of beauty and class, whose voice no one had ever heard. Encomia were devoted to the noble intelligence of her expression. Her photograph was displayed on the covers of several magazines. In black and white, in colour, it didn't matter, she looked wonderful in all of them.

Zdena read an editorial devoted to the glory of 'the beautiful CKZ 114'.

Beautiful: so that was it. Kapo Zdena hadn't dared put it into words, on the basis that she didn't know anything about it. She was quite proud to have been capable, if not of understanding, then at least of noticing the phenomenon.

Beauty: so that was CKZ 114's problem. The supposedly beautiful girls on television hadn't provoked that unease in Zdena, who therefore concluded that perhaps they weren't really beautiful after all. *Concentration* taught her the meaning of true beauty.

She cut out a particularly good photograph of CKZ 114 and stuck it up near her bed.

*

One thing the inmates had in common with the viewers was the fact that they knew the names of the kapos. And the kapos in turn never missed an opportunity to yell out their own identities, as though they felt a need to hear them.

During the morning selection, one would hear:

'Stand up straight in the presence of Kapo Marko!'

Or when working on the tunnel:

'Is that what you call obeying Kapo Jan?'

There was a certain equality among the kapos, not least in their wickedness, brutality and stupidity.

The kapos were young. None of them was more than thirty. There had been no shortage of older candidates, even of quite elderly ones. But the organisers had thought that blind violence would be more impressive if it emanated from youthful bodies, adolescent muscles and chubby faces.

There was even one freakish character, Kapo Lenka, a luscious vamp who was perpetually trying to please. It wasn't enough for her to attract the viewer and swing her hips in front of the other kapos: she went so far as to try and seduce the prisoners, thrusting her cleavage in their faces and making eyes at those she subjugated. This nymphomania, along with the rancid atmosphere that was rife in the programme, was as repellent as it was fascinating.

The inmates also had this in common with the viewers: they didn't know the names of their comrades in misfortune. They would have liked to know them, for sympathy and friendship were indispensable to them; and yet an instinct alerted them to the danger of such knowledge.

They soon received a serious illustration of this.

Kapo Zdena sought out every opportunity to be in the presence of the young CKZ 114. The instructions hadn't changed: if she had to beat someone gratuitously, it should be the beautiful girl.

Fired by this task, Zdena could invoke duty to take out her fury on Pannonique. She put a special zeal into this. Without transgressing her orders, which were not to damage her beauty, the kapo thrashed CKZ 114 more than she really needed to.

The organisers had noticed this. They didn't disapprove of her tendency: there was something telegenic in seeing this incarnation of abrasiveness that was Zdena lashing out at the girl's heartrending delicacy.

They had not attributed too much importance to another sign of the kapo's obsession: she constantly named, or rather numbered, her victim. It was always:

'Get up, CKZ 114!'

Or:

'I'll teach you about obedience, CKZ 114!'

Or:

'You'll see what's coming to you, CKZ 114!'

Or indeed this simple, telling shout:

'CKZ 114!'

Sometimes, when she could not beat the young body any more, she threw it to the ground, whispering:

'We'll leave it there for the time being, CKZ!'

In the face of this treatment, Pannonique's courage and manners remained thoroughly admirable. She didn't unclench her teeth, and she stifled even the faintest moans of pain.

In Pannonique's unit, there was a man of about thirty who was driven mad by this torment. He would a thousand times rather have been beaten himself than witness the girl's recurrent torture. During break, one evening, the man, called EPJ 327, came to talk to her:

'She's hounding you, CKZ 114. It's unbearable.'

'If it wasn't her, it would be someone else.'

'I'd rather it was someone else who was being beaten.'

'What do you expect me to do, EPJ 327?'

'I don't know. Do you want me to speak to her?'

'You know you aren't allowed to, and it would only aggravate her violence.'

'Couldn't you speak to her?'

'I have no more rights than you do.'

'We don't know that. Kapo Zdena's obsessed with you.'

'Do you think I want to play her game?'

'I see what you mean.'

They spoke in very low voices, for fear that one of the omnipresent microphones might capture their conversation.

'CKZ 114, can I ask you your first name?'

'In other circumstances I'd have loved to tell you. But now I think it would be very unwise.'

'Why? If you like, I'm prepared to reveal to you that I'm called . . .'

'EPJ 327. You're called EPJ 327.'

'That's harsh. I need you to know my name. And I need to know yours.'

He was starting to raise his voice, despairingly. She put a finger to his lips. He shivered.

In fact, Kapo Zdena's passion intersected with that of EPJ 327: she too was burning to know CKZ 114's first name. After roaring that number forty times a day, she was coming to find it unsatisfactory.

Not for nothing do human beings bear names rather than numbers: the first name is the key to the personality. It is the delicate click of the lock when you want to open the door. It's the metallic music that makes the gift possible.

The number is to knowledge of the other what the identity card is to the person: precisely nothing.

Zdena was furious to notice this limit to her power: she, who had such extensive and monstrous rights over inmate CKZ 114, had no means of discovering her name. It was not recorded anywhere: the prisoners' papers were burned the moment they arrived at the camp.

She could only learn CKZ 114's name from her own lips.

Unsure whether her question was permitted, Zdena approached the girl cautiously during the work on the tunnel, and whispered in her ear:

'What's your name?'

Pannonique turned a startled face towards her.

'What's your name?' the kapo murmured again.

CKZ 114 gave a definitive shake of the head. And she started clearing stones again.

Defeated, Zdena took her bludgeon and laid into the insolent girl. When she was finally too exhausted to continue, her victim, in spite of her pain, shot her an amused glance that seemed to say, 'Do you really imagine you're going to weaken me like that?'

I'm an idiot, the kapo thought. In order to get what I want, I'm destroying her. You stupid cow, Zdena! And it isn't my fault, either: she taunts me, she infuriates me, so I lose it. She got no more than she deserved!

Watching unedited tapes, Zdena saw that CKZ 114 had had a conversation with EPJ 327. She pilfered some sodium pentothal from the infirmary, and injected EPJ 327 with a dose of it. The truth drug loosened the tongue of the unfortunate man, who started speaking profusely.

'My name is Pietro, Pietro Livi, I so needed to say it, I so need to know the name of CKZ 114, she was right to hide it from me, otherwise I would be telling it to you now, Kapo Zdena, I hate you, you are all that I despise, and CKZ 114 is all that I love, beauty, nobility, grace, if I could kill you, Kapo Zdena . . .'

Reckoning that she had heard enough, she knocked him out. Some organisers intercepted her: she was not permitted to torture the prisoners for her own selfish pleasure.

'Do what you want, Kapo Zdena, but do it in front of the cameras.'

The sodium pentothal was confiscated.

If I wasn't the queen of all cretins, thought Zdena, I would have injected that sodium pentothal into CKZ 114. Now, I won't be able to get my hands on it, and I won't know her name. They were right, what they said in that newspaper: I'm stupidity personified.

It was the first time in her life that Zdena became aware and ashamed of her worthlessness.

*

At flogging time, she took turns with other kapos. There was no shortage of brutes willing to vent their fury on the frail body of CKZ 114.

Initially, Zdena felt she was making progress. She didn't feel too much of a need to destroy the thing that was obsessing her. Sometimes she struck other prisoners so as not to look as if she was twiddling her thumbs. But it didn't matter.

Gradually, her conscience came to trouble her. How could she be pleased with herself over such a trifle? CKZ 114 was being subjected to just as much violence as before. Washing your hands of a situation didn't make you innocent.

A hidden part of Zdena whispered to her that when she was the one hounding CKZ 114, there was something holy about her actions. While now the girl was subjected to the common fate, blind horror, ordinary torture.

Kapo Zdena decided to reassert her status as the chosen one. She started beating the living daylights out of the young beauty once again. When the girl saw her tormentor coming back after a week's break, her eyes were filled with a perplexity that seemed to ask the meaning of such strange behaviour.

Zdena started asking her question again:

'What's your name?'

And again she refused to tell her, without relinquishing that wry expression which the kapo correctly read as: 'Do you imagine that I see your return as an act of grace for which I should thank you?'

She's right, thought Zdena. I must give her a reason for satisfaction.

EPJ 327 told CKZ 114 about the interrogation to which he had been subjected.

'You see,' she said, 'I mustn't let you know my name.'

'She knows mine now, but clearly nobody cares about that. You are Kapo Zdena's sole obsession.'

'That's a privilege I could happily do without.'

'I'm sure you could use it to your own advantage.'

'I would rather not understand what you mean.'

'I didn't mean it in a derogatory way. You have no idea of my esteem for you. And I am grateful to you for inspiring it in me: never in my life have I needed to hold someone in such high esteem as I do now that we are in this inferno.'

'And I have never had such a need to hold my head high. It's the only thing that keeps me going.'

'Thank you. Your pride is mine. I have a sense that it's the pride of everyone else here, too.'

He was not mistaken. The eyes of the other prisoners were also magnetised by her beauty.

'Did you know that the most sublime words ever written about the glories of the dramatist Corneille were written by a French Jew in 1940?' EPJ 327 continued.

'Were you a teacher?' Pannonique asked.

'I still am. I refuse to talk about it in the past tense.'

'So, Kapo Zdena, you've started beating up CKZ again?' laughed Kapo Jan.

'Yes,' she said, failing to notice that she was being made fun of.

'You like her, don't you?' asked Kapo Marko.

'I do,' she replied.

'You love whacking her. You can't do without it.'

Zdena thought very quickly. Her instinct told her to lie.

'Yes, I like it.'

The others laughed loudly.

Zdena reflected that two weeks before, it wouldn't have been a lie.

'Can I ask a favour of you guys?' she inquired.

'Ask away.'

'Leave her to me.'

The kapos yelled with laughter.

'Fine, Kapo Zdena, you can have her,' said Kapo Jan. 'On one condition.'

'What's that?' asked Zdena.

'That you tell us about it.'

The next day, at work on the tunnel, CKZ 114 saw Kapo Zdena coming towards her with her cudgel in her hand.

The camera trained on the pair of girls with whom the viewers were obsessed.

Pannonique tried extra hard, even though she knew her zeal would get her nowhere.

'You're a wimp, CKZ 114!' bellowed the kapo.

Cudgel-blows rained down upon the prisoner.

Pannonique immediately noticed that she didn't feel a thing. The cudgel had been replaced by a harmless imitation. CKZ 114's reflex was to feign mute suffering.

Then she glanced briefly at the kapo's face. In it she saw a meaningful intensity: her tormentor was responsible for this new development, and she wasn't going to let her victim in on the secret.

The very next moment, Zdena turned once more into an ordinary kapo, roaring her hatred.

After a week of fake blows, Kapo Zdena asked CKZ 114 her question again:

'What's your name?'

Pannonique didn't reply. Her eyes plumbed her enemy's. She took her share of rubble and brought it to the common pile. Then she came back to refill her container.

Zdena was waiting for her, an insistent expression on her face, as though to tell her that her favouritism deserved a reward.

'What are you called?'

Pannonique thought for a moment before saying:

'I'm called CKZ 114.'

It was the first time that a kapo had heard her speak.

Rather than give Zdena her name, she was giving her an unexpected gift: the sound of her voice. A sound that was sober, severe and pure. A voice with an uncommon timbre.

So disconcerted was Zdena that she didn't notice the biased reply.

The kapo wasn't the only one to notice the phenomenon. The next day, several columnists wrote under the headline SHE HAS SPOKEN!

It was extremely rare for a prisoner to speak. More to the point, no media had ever before captured the voice of CKZ 114. All that had ever been heard from her were vague groans as the blows rained down upon her. Now she had said something:

'I'm called CKZ 114.'

'The most unusual thing about this statement,' one journalist wrote, 'is the word *I*. So, this girl who, before our disconcerted eyes, is undergoing the worst cruelty imaginable, dehumanisation, humiliation, total violence – this girl whose death we will witness, who is already dead, can still proudly begin a sentence with a triumphant *I*, a self-affirmation. What a lesson in courage!'

Another newspaper drew the opposite analysis:

'This girl is publicly proclaiming her defeat. She is – finally! – speaking, but only to admit that she has been defeated, to say that the only identity by which she recognises herself now is the number imposed upon her by this barbaric horror.'

None of the media grasped the true nature of what had happened: the action had only taken place between these two girls, and had meaning for them alone. And that huge meaning was: 'I agree to enter into talks with you.'

The other inmates didn't understand any more than the media. They all felt the greatest admiration for CKZ 114. She was their heroine, the one whose nobility gave them the courage to hold their heads high.

A young woman bearing the number MDA 802 said to Pannonique:

'It's good that you're holding out on her.'

The young woman had used the familiar *tu*.

'If you don't mind,' Pannonique replied, 'I'd rather we called each other *vous*.'

'I thought we were friends.'

'Exactly. Let's leave *tu* for the people who want to hurt us.'

'It'll be difficult for me to do that. You and I are the same age.'

'The kapos are our age too. It's the proof that, once childhood is over, having the same age is no longer a point in common.'

'Do you think using *vous* will get us anywhere?'

'Anything that distinguishes us from the kapos is utterly indispensable. As is everything which reminds us that, unlike them, we are civilised individuals.'

The attitude spread. Soon all the prisoners were addressing each other in the polite form.

There were consequences to this. They didn't like each

26

other any the less, they were no less intimate with one another, but they respected each other infinitely more. It wasn't a formal deference: it was more that they held each other in greater esteem.

The evening meal was wretched: stale bread and soup so clear that it would have been a miracle if your bowl contained so much as a piece of vegetable peel. But they were so hungry, and the helpings were so small, that they still waited feverishly for this collation.

On receiving their fare, the inmates threw themselves on it without a word, and ate it sparingly, weakly, eking out their mouthfuls.

Often, at the end of their ration, someone would burst out sobbing at the idea of having so empty a belly until the following evening: having lived only for this pathetic meal, and having no hope of anything, was enough to make you cry.

Pannonique couldn't bear that suffering. During one meal she started talking. Like a guest around a well-laid table, she fell into conversation with the members of her unit. She talked about the films she had loved, and the actors she admired. One neighbour agreed, the next one waxed indignant and contradicted her, and put his point of view. Voices were raised. Everyone adopted a position. They became passionate. Pannonique burst out laughing.

Only EPJ 327 noticed.

'It's the first time I've seen you laugh.'

'I'm laughing with happiness. They're talking, they're arguing, as though it was important. It's wonderful!'

'You're the one who's wonderful. Thanks to you, they've forgotten they were eating crap.'

'Not you?'

'This isn't the first time I've noticed your power. Without you I'd be dead.'

27

'People don't die as easily as that.'

'There's nothing easier than dying here. You just have to prove incapable of work, and the next day you're killed.'

'But you can't decide you're going to die.'

'Yes, you can. It's called suicide.'

'Very few human beings are truly capable of suicide. I'm like most people, I have a survival instinct. So do you.'

'Quite honestly, without you I'm not sure that I would have. Even in my previous life, I've never known anyone like you: someone you can devote your thoughts to. I have only to think of you and I'm saved from disgust.'

There were no more squalid meals at Pannonique's table. The surrounding units grasped the principle and imitated it: now no one ate in silence. The refectory became a noisy place.

They were still as hungry as before, yet no one burst out sobbing as they finished their meagre fare.

And still they went on losing weight. CKZ 114, who had been thin when she arrived at the camp, had lost the sweet roundness of her cheeks. This enhanced the beauty of her eyes, but the beauty of her body deteriorated.

Kapo Zdena grew worried. She tried to slip food to the girl who obsessed her. CKZ 114 refused it, horrified at the idea of the risk she would run by accepting it.

Either Zdena's gesture would be recorded by the camera, and CKZ 114 risk a punishment the nature of which she preferred not to know.

Or else Zdena's gesture would not be recorded by the camera, in which case CKZ 114 preferred not to think how the kapo would expect her to show her gratitude.

Besides, she was dying of hunger. It was terrible to be

given bars of chocolate the very thought of which made her sick with desire. But still she kept her resolve for want of an answer.

It just so happened that MDA 802 noticed what was going on. At break time, in a low voice, she came to abuse her companion in misfortune:

'How dare you refuse food?'

'That's my business, MDA 802.'

'No, it's our business too. You could share that chocolate.'

'All you have to do is go with Kapo Zdena.'

'You know very well she's only interested in you.'

'Don't you think I have grounds to complain?'

'No. We all want someone to come and give us chocolate.'

'At what price, MDA 802?'

'A price fixed by you, CKZ 114.'

And she left, furious.

Pannonique thought. MDA 802 had a point. She had been selfish. 'A price fixed by you': yes, there must be a way of manoeuvring without surrendering.

Zdena was incapable of thinking with the words that EPJ 327 had used. But the phenomena she witnessed within her own head were not dissimilar. She knew the disgust he had mentioned to Pannonique. She felt it intensely enough to call it by its name.

Since her earliest youth, whenever Zdena was despised, when other people in her presence despised things they didn't understand, when they gratuitously demolished something beautiful, when someone was belittled for the self-indulgent, mud-wallowing pleasure of humiliation, she felt a persistent unease that her brain had identified as disgust.

She had grown used to living with this filth, telling herself that it was the human condition, even nourishing it to give herself the illusion that she herself was not always the victim. She thought it was better to provoke revulsion than to be subjected to it.

On very rare occasions, the disgust faded away. When she heard a piece of music that struck her as beautiful, when she left a stuffy room and felt the sheer generosity of fresh, icy air, when the satiety of a banquet was forgotten in a sip of flinty wine, it was better than a respite: suddenly disgust was erased and there was no word for its opposite, it was neither appetite nor desire, it was a thousand times stronger, a faith in something too vast that spread within her until her eyes popped.

Pannonique had this effect on her. A nameless sensation

for a nameless person: there was too much namelessness in this whole affair. No matter what the cost, Zdena would get hold of CKZ 114's first name.

Weight loss was not so much an aesthetic problem as a matter of life and death. The inmates were given their first inspection in the morning: those who looked too emaciated to be viable were selected for the 'bad line'.

Some prisoners slipped rags underneath their uniforms to pad out their bodies. The idea of losing too much weight was a constant source of anxiety.

A unit consisted of ten people. Pannonique was obsessed by the health of these ten individuals, which included EPJ 327 and MDA 802. But the unconscious pressure that her unit exerted upon her to accept the kapo's chocolate was becoming unbearable.

The horror of circumstances inflamed her pride. My name is worth more than chocolate, she thought.

Meanwhile she too was losing weight. Being the public's muse didn't shield her from death: the organisers were already rubbing their hands at the idea of the telegenic nature of her death-throes being broadcast by five cameras.

Zdena panicked. Since CKZ 114 persisted in refusing the chocolate she offered her, the kapo imperiously slipped it into the pocket of her overalls. The girl immediately gestured to her to repeat the action. Zdena was so flabbergasted by such impudence that, unseen by everyone, she slipped a second bar into her protégée's pocket.

The girl gave her a vague wink of thanks. Zdena couldn't get over such grandeur. 'She really thinks she's something,' she said to herself. But she was convinced that the girl was perfectly right.

At dinnertime Pannonique slipped bars of chocolate from knee to knee under the table, unleashing a wave of touching enthusiasm. The prisoners devoured the booty with ecstasy.

'Was it Kapo Zdena who gave it to you?' asked MDA 802.

'Yes.'

EPJ 327 grimaced at the idea of what CKZ 114 must have paid for it.

'What price did you agree?' MDA 802 persisted.

'None. I got the chocolate for nothing.'

EPJ 327 sighed with relief.

'She values your life,' observed MDA 802.

'You see, I was right not to waste my name,' said CKZ 114.

There was a general explosion of laughter.

It became a habit: each day the kapo slipped two bars of chocolate into CKZ 114's pocket, receiving only a swift glance by way of thanks.

After her initial shock, Zdena started to think that her protégée was taking her for a ride. She loved the idea of playing benefactor to her obsession. And yet Pannonique showed no sign of being overwhelmed with gratitude: if at least she had turned big eyes filled with appreciation towards Zdena! As it was, the girl behaved as though the chocolate were her due. Zdena said to herself that CKZ 114 was going a bit far. As the days passed, her resentment grew. She felt as if she was experiencing a humiliation that was all too familiar to her: she was despised.

She knew by now that the kapos and the public despised her: she didn't care about that. But CKZ 114's contempt made her ill. She regretted swapping her cudgel for a harmless substitute. She would have liked to give the girl a really good thrashing.

And worse: she felt as if the whole of CKZ 114's unit despised her. She must have been their laughing-stock. She thought of depriving the girl of chocolate. Sadly, she hadn't put on any weight.

Clearly she must have been sharing the chocolate with the others. That was why it was doing her no good. Those bastards in her unit might even be taking her share. And they were making fun of her, on top of everything.

Zdena was filled with boundless hatred of the group that surrounded her obsession.

The kapo's revenge was not long in coming.

One morning when she was inspecting her protégée's unit, Zdena stopped in front of MDA 802.

She took her time, saying nothing, knowing how terrifying her silence was for her victim. She looked her up and down. Was it because of her pointy, impertinent little face, in a sense the opposite of her own? Was it because she felt she was friends with CKZ 114? Zdena hated MDA 802.

The whole unit held its breath, sharing the unfortunate's fate.

'You're thin, MDA 802,' the kapo said finally.

'No, I'm not, Kapo Zdena,' the rebel replied.

'Yes, you are, you've lost weight. How couldn't you be losing weight, with forced labour and a famine diet?'

'I haven't lost weight, Kapo Zdena.'

34

'You haven't lost weight? Has someone been giving you sweets in secret?'

'No, Kapo Zdena,' said the prisoner, increasingly sick with fear.

'Yes, they have, don't deny that you've lost weight!' yelled the kapo.

And she grabbed the inmate by the shoulder and hurled her like a projectile into the line of condemned prisoners. MDA 802's chin started trembling convulsively.

It was then that the inexpressible thing took place.

CKZ 114 left her line, gripped MDA 802's hand and brought her back among the living.

And as Zdena furiously ran over to enforce her death sentence, CKZ 114 plonked herself in front of her, plunged her eyes into the kapo's and loudly proclaimed:

'My name is Pannonique!'

Part Two

An eternity passed before things resumed their course.

Zdena stood motionless before the girl, who was now more fully named than anyone else. Blessed, astounded, scandalised, dazed, she had received a direct blow to the head.

MDA 802, utterly shattered, wept soundlessly.

CKZ 114 didn't take her eyes off the kapo. She looked her up and down with extreme intensity.

Overcome, EPJ 327 contemplated her. He found her as magnificent as her first name.

In the room with the ninety-five screens, the organisers were exultant.

The girl had a sense of showmanship. They weren't completely sure they had understood what had happened; they were sure, however, that the audience *hadn't* understood, given how contemptible they were. And they were equally certain that the scene would become legendary.

Other media were already phoning to inquire about the significance of the event. They were told that it didn't fall within the rules of the game: young CKZ 114 had created a shock whose value lay solely in its uniqueness. It was a happening. Which meant that it wouldn't happen again.

Their response was all the more abrupt because they failed to grasp the nature of the miracle.

*

Who did grasp it?

Not Zdena, who had abandoned the realms of reason. Too dazzled by what she had heard to think, she was still being affected by the identity of the girl who obsessed her. She felt faint.

Not CKZ 114, who thought she had hit by chance upon a useful device. My name has saved a life. A name is worth a life. If each of us becomes aware of the price of his first name and behaves accordingly, many lives will be spared.

Not the other prisoners who, while they might have been deeply moved, thought they had witnessed a sacrifice, a defeat. Their heroine had parted with a treasure to save a friend. Wasn't that the start of prostitution? Did this gift not expose her to more serious offerings?

EPJ 327 alone understood: he knew that this act could not be repeated. When a name is a rampart and its impregnability intoxicates, it's called love. What they had witnessed was an act of love.

The terrible thing about miracles is the limit of their impact.

The strike force of the name Pannonique saved the life of MDA 802 and showed the kapo the existence of the sacred. But it didn't save those who were killed by *Concentration* that day, and neither did it reveal the existence of the sacred to anyone else.

Nor did it stop time from pressing on. The exhausted, starving prisoners went to work on the tunnel under a rain of cudgel-blows. Despair took hold of them once more.

Some of them were astonished to hear themselves thinking, to fire their own courage: Her name is Pannonique. They weren't sure what it was in that information that was able to give them such strength, but they observed that it did.

At dinner, CKZ 114 was welcomed like a heroine. The whole refectory chanted her name when she came in.

There was a lively atmosphere at her unit's table.

'I'm sorry,' she began. 'Kapo Zdena didn't give me any chocolate today.'

'Thanks, Pannonique. You've saved my life,' MDA 802 said solemnly.

CKZ 114 threw herself into the theory that she had mentally constructed while working on the tunnel. She explained that everyone could and should do as she had: in that way, they could bring plenty of condemned inmates back to the line of the living.

They listened to her politely. They still weren't going to tell her that she was talking nonsense.

When she had finished her enthusiastic speech, EPJ 327 declared:

'Whatever else happens, we will only ever call you Pannonique, isn't that right?'

There was general agreement.

'It's a lovely name, I'd never heard it before,' said a man who spoke seldom.

'For me, it will always be the loveliest name in the world,' said MDA 802.

'For all of us, your name will be the noblest of all for eternity,' said EPJ 327.

'I don't know where to put myself,' said CKZ 114.

'Romain Gary was a prisoner in a German camp during the last war,' EPJ 327 continued. 'The conditions of survival for the inmates were more or less the same as ours. I don't

41

need to tell you how inhuman it was and, worse, dehumanising. Unlike here, the sexes were separated. In his men's camp, Gary saw the inmates, like himself, becoming little savages. Their thoughts were a tragedy yet more serious than what they endured. Their worst torment was when they were conscious. Constantly cheated out of the meanest portion of humanity to which they had been reduced, they aspired to death. Until the day when one of them had a brilliant idea: he invented the character of the lady.'

EPJ 327 broke off to remove a floating cockroach from his soup, then continued:

'He decided that from now on they would all live as though there were a lady among them, a real one, who would be addressed with all the honours due to such a person, and before whom they were afraid of demeaning themselves. This imaginative construction was adopted by everyone. And so it happened. Gradually, they realised that they were saved: by living in the elevated company of the fictional lady, they had rebuilt civilisation. At their meals, where their food was not much better than ours, they started talking again, or rather conversing, holding dialogues, listening attentively to one another. They spoke respectfully to the lady, telling her things that were worthy of her. Even when they didn't speak to her, they became accustomed to the idea of living beneath her gaze, behaving in such a way that her eyes would not be upset. This fresh fervour did not escape the kapos, who heard mutterings about the presence of a lady and held an investigation. They searched the camp from top to bottom and didn't find anyone. This mental victory on the part of the prisoners sustained them to the end.'

'That's a lovely story,' said one of the inmates.

'Ours is even lovelier,' replied EPJ 327. 'We didn't need to invent our character of the lady: she exists, she lives with us, we can look at her, talk to her, she answers us, she saves us and her name is Pannonique.'

'I'm sure an imaginary lady would be much more effective,' murmured CKZ 114.

EPJ 327 had forgotten to mention another fundamental way in which their camp differed from the Nazi camps: the cameras. His omission was significant: the prisoners very soon stopped thinking about them. They were too preoccupied by their suffering to present themselves as a spectacle.

That partial amnesia saved them. While the benevolent gaze of an imaginary lady or a real girl helped them to live, the cold and voracious eye of the machine reduced them to slavery. Worse: it reduced the fictitious possibilities of the spirit.

Any human being who experiences a lasting or a passing hell can, in order to confront it, resort to the most gratifying mental technique in existence: he can tell himself a story. The exploited worker invents himself as a prisoner-of-war, the prisoner-of-war imagines himself a Grail hunter, and so on. Every form of wretchedness has its own emblem and its own heroism. The poor wretch who can inflate his chest with a breath of greatness holds his head up high and ceases to complain.

Unless he notices the camera spying on his pain. He knows then that the audience will see him as a victim rather than a tragic fighter.

Crushed in advance by the idiot box, he drops the epic weapons of his interior narrative. And he becomes what people will see: a poor unfortunate crushed by an external story, a mean portion of himself.

It is when his absence is most glaring that God is most necessary. Before *Concentration*, God was to Pannonique what he was to most people: an idea. Interesting to contemplate, exciting to imagine its dizzy heights. As to the concept of divine love, it was particularly fascinating, so much so as to lead one to forget the notorious question of the existence of God: the ancient practice of apologetics yielded nothing but nonsense.

Since her arrest, Pannonique had had a terrible need for God. She hungered to insult him until her throat was dry. If only she could have held a superior presence responsible for this inferno, she would have had the comfort of being able to hate it with all her strength, to make it the target of her most violent imprecations. Sadly, the incontestable reality of the camp was the denial of God: the existence of one led ineluctably to the non-existence of the other. It was impossible even to think about it: the absence of God was beyond discussion.

It was unbearable to have no one to direct such hatred against. From this state was there born a form of madness? Hating humanity? There was no point in that. Humanity was that disparate swarm, that ludicrous supermarket that sold everything and its opposite. To hate humanity was to hate a universal encyclopaedia. That was an irremediable execration.

No, what Pannonique needed to hate was the founding principle. One day, something slipped into her head: since

44

the post was vacant, she, Pannonique, would be God.

At first she laughed at the outrageousness of her plan. Her laughter held her back: already, the very fact of having found a reason to laugh impressed her. The plan was aberrant and grotesque, certainly: she didn't care. In terms of aberration, she could go no further than this camp.

God: she wasn't cut out for the role. No one was. But that wasn't the issue. The post was vacant: that was the problem. So she would fill that post. She would be the founding principle to be hated: it was much less painful than having no one to direct your hatred against. But it wouldn't stop there. She would be God in her head, and not just in order to rail against herself.

She would be God in every respect. It was no longer a matter of creating the universe: too late, damage done. Basically, once creation was accomplished, what was the task of God? Probably that of a writer when his book is published: publicly to love his text, to receive compliments, jeers and indifference on its behalf. To confront certain readers who denounce the work's shortcomings when, even if they are right, it would be impossible to change it. To love it to the bitter end. That love was the sole concrete help that one would be able to bring to it.

All the more reason to say nothing. Pannonique thought of those novelists who go on endlessly about the book they've written: what's the point? Wouldn't they have served their book better if they had, at the moment of its creation, injected it with all the love it needed? And if they had failed to give it that support at the appropriate moment, wouldn't they have done their text more good by loving it anyway, with that true love expressed not in logorrhoea but in silence punctuated by a few fine words? Creation wasn't so hard, because it was intoxicating: only once it was over did the

45

divine task became complicated.

That was where Pannonique would intervene. She wouldn't be Christ – no question of playing expiatory victims, the role assigned to them by the programme. She would be God, the principle of greatness and love.

In concrete terms, this meant truly loving the others. And that wouldn't be a simple matter, because it was far from the case that all the others inspired love.

Loving MDA 802 and EPJ 327 – what could be more natural than that? Loving the inmates you knew nothing about wasn't complicated either. Loving the ones who were tiresome to those around them was still a possibility. You can love someone as long as you can understand them.

But how was Pannonique going to be able to love ZHF 911?

ZHF 911 was an old woman. It was curious that the organisers hadn't yet eliminated this woman, since they normally killed all old people as a matter of course. Nonetheless, it was easy to guess why they kept her: because she was revolting.

She was a Fairy Carabosse, her face furrowed with the thousand wrinkles of perversity. Her mouth expressed evil both with its pleated shape – the characteristic creases of malevolent lips – and with the words that emerged from them: she always found people's flaws, which enabled her to wound them. The damage she did was entirely verbal: she was living proof of the baleful power of language.

Even in the train bringing the prisoners to the camp, ZHF 911 had drawn attention to herself: to mothers pressing children to their breasts, the old woman announced the fate that awaited their offspring. 'It's obvious,' she said. 'The Nazis exterminated the little ones first. And you can see why: bawling little squirts, all pee and poo, nothing but trouble, and the ingratitude of them! Don't get too attached to them, they'll be killed as soon as we get there. Well, my dear madam, apart from thickening your waist, what have the brats done for you?'

Utterly flabbergasted, the mothers didn't know what to say to this monster. Some men had broken in:

'Listen, you old hag, you know what happened to senior citizens in Dachau?'

'That's what we're about to find out,' she had screeched.

The woman who was not yet called ZHF 911 had not been mistaken: the cameras in the trucks must have captured her character because, upon arrival at the camp, she was spared, unlike the other old people. The organisers must have thought that she would undermine the morale of the inmates, and that that would be amusing. Was that what she had premeditated? Nothing could be less certain. It quickly became apparent that this woman didn't give a damn about anything.

To study ZHF 911 was to study evil. Her chief characteristic was her complete indifference: she was neither for the kapos, nor for the prisoners, nor for herself. She was no more attached to herself than she was to anyone else. The idea of defending anyone or anything struck her as utterly grotesque. If she liked telling everybody awful things, it was without any underlying plan: only for the simple pleasure of causing them pain.

ZHF 911's scientific observation revealed other aspects of evil: she was inert, she had no energy for anything but speech – but her energy was unparalleled. If she gave the impression of intelligence, it was because of the wickedness of her rejoinders, which spread tears and despair.

It was terrible to realise that the worst creature around was to be found among the inmates and not on the side of evil. This was logical: the devil divides. ZHF 911 was what caused the camp to ossify; without her, it would have been nothing but a pitiful clutch of human beings torn apart by internecine quarrels.

How could the prisoners have imagined they were on the side of good when each morning they hoped for the death of the despicable old woman? When the kapos came to remove the day's condemned from the line, the fear of being chosen was mingled with the wish that ZHF 911 might be. She never was. After the inspection had spared her once again, she would give her camp a look of triumph. She knew how much her elimination was yearned for.

Some kind souls waxed indignant about the hatred heaped on her: 'Look, she's a very old lady, she's not quite right in the head, how can you hate her? It isn't her fault.' These comments provoked arguments that reached the ears of ZHF 911 and delighted her. 'They might actually get on quite well without me,' she said to herself.

The snake-tongued gossip also poured her venom on the kapos (always going for the wounding word: so Kapo Lenka wasn't called a slut, which might have made her smile, but a desperate old hag, which made her furious), the organisers – 'little Nazis', the 'poor man's Hitlers' – and the viewers, who were referred to as 'big fat sheep'. No one could stand her.

However, the worst thing she did could not be held against her, because she wasn't aware that she was doing it: ZHF 911 howled at the moon. Almost every night, at about midnight, shrill ululations were heard rising from the camp; the performance lasted five minutes and then subsided. It took people a while to work out the source of the cries. The inmates who slept in the same hut as the old woman finally denounced her: 'Deliver us from this madwoman, who has not a scrap of humanity.'

The bosses rubbed their hands. They organised coverage of this nocturnal nuisance: first of all the camp was shown asleep, and all of a sudden a terrible wailing was heard, the camera seemed to be searching, it entered a hut and ZHF 911 could be made out sitting on her mattress and groaning. A few minutes later she was seen falling back unconscious on to her bed.

The phenomenon was investigated. ZHF 911 looked sincerely astonished and denied everything.

Nothing undermined the prisoners' morale as much as these manifestations of pure insanity. When the wails rang out, each inmate thought furiously: 'Let them kill her! Let them take her from the line tomorrow morning!'

Pannonique was dying of hatred for this woman, and dreaming of her demise. However much she might try and reason, tell herself that it was not ZHF 911 who had set up *Concentration*, she felt her fingernails turning into talons as soon as she saw her. And when she heard the pest bellowing at night, she longed to strangle her with her own bare hands.

'How easy it would be to be God if ZHF 911 did not exist!' She laughed at the absurdity of her thought: in fact, it would be easy to be God if evil didn't exist – but in that case you wouldn't need God either.

At the opposite extreme, there was in the camp a little girl who, strangely, had been spared. PFX 150 was twelve, and there was nothing unusual about her. She didn't look especially advanced for her age, she was quite cute without being pretty, and her dazed expression spoke of her innocence. She was a nice child who didn't say much. She couldn't understand why she hadn't been killed, and didn't know if it wouldn't have been better that way.

'What's keeping them from liquidating that kid?' ZHF 911 said at the top of her voice whenever their paths crossed.

PFX 150, who was probably well brought-up, gave no reply. Pannonique seethed with rage.

'Why don't you defend yourself?' she asked the child.

'Because she isn't speaking to me.'

Pannonique taught her a phrase to say out loud the next time ZHF 911 launched off on her tirade.

This happened shortly afterwards. PFX 150 raised her thin voice to declaim:

'What's keeping them from ridding us of that old woman who howls at the moon?'

ZHF 911 smiled.

'Quite,' she replied. 'I know why they're keeping me: it's because I'm spoiling your lives, which are quite horrible enough already. But you're insignificant, you don't bother anyone, for what vile reason are they keeping you alive?'

Stupefied, the girl could find nothing to say. When

Pannonique came to congratulate her for having spoken, PFX 150 hitback:

'Leave me alone! I was right to remain silent! Because of you, I gave her the opportunity to say even worse things to me! And now I'm sick with fear. Keep your nose out of other people's business!'

Pannonique tried to take the child in her arms to comfort her: she broke violently away.

'You give yourself such airs, as though you had the answer to everything; but it's not true, you only make things worse,' the girl stormed.

Pannonique was mortified. 'That'll teach me to credit myself with powers I don't have,' she thought.

Nonetheless, she didn't give up her inner divinity, and resolved to find a better use for it.

Pannonique was woken by the wails of ZHF 911, as she was almost every night.

Why do I hate her more for her cries than for the muck she throws at us? Why am I incapable of being fair?

The fact was that the whole camp shared her attitude; the old woman's madness was more upsetting than her wickedness. It is true that the latter quality did not lack an unintentional comedy, while her nocturnal cries merely underlined the squalor of their present existence. Pannonique tried to analyse the ululations – the word suddenly struck her as ill-chosen. The song of the owl is not without its charms. The noise made by the old woman was more like the long howl of a mastiff. It rose, peaked, fell, stopped and started all over again.

After about five minutes, a hoarse spasm ('Aaaah!') announced that it was over.

Pannonique felt like smiling. The artist has finished his show and takes leave of his audience.

Then she thought she heard something. Oh, no, she's starting up again! But as she pricked up her ears she frowned: it had nothing to do with it. It wasn't the old woman's voice, it was the plaintive chirping of a human sparrow.

It stopped very quickly. But that tiny cry haunted Pannonique. It tore her heart apart.

The next day, she asked around on the sly. But no one had heard anything other than the old woman's lamentations. Even so, she still didn't feel reassured.

While she slaved to clear away the rubble, she felt a rush of hatred as she thought of the viewers. It was a slow implosion that started in her ribcage and rose to her teeth, turning them into fangs. To think that they're out there, slumped in front of the box, savouring the hell we're in and doubtless pretending to be indignant about it! Not one of them has actually come to save us, that goes without saying, but it doesn't surprise me: not one has switched off his television or changed channels, I'd bet my life on it.

Kapo Zdena came over to rain down cudgel-blows on her, hurling abuse, then went to busy herself elsewhere.

I hate her too, and yet I hate her much less than I hate the audience. I prefer the one who beats me to the ones who watch me on the receiving end of her aggression. She isn't hypocritical; she's openly playing an odious role. There's a hierarchy of evil, and Kapo Zdena isn't the one who occupies the most repellent place in it.

She saw Kapo Marko shouting at PFX 150. Her status as a child meant fewer blows and more verbal punishment. She seemed at a loss. What she was experiencing reminded her of school, where adults yelled at her, and at the same time it didn't remind her of anything, but an undertow of girlish submission still stifled all spirit of revolt.

Pannonique went surreptitiously over to her.

'What was he saying to you?' she asked the girl, using the formal 'vous'.

'I was pretending to listen.'

'Well done,' said Pannonique, who thought that childhood had its own resources.

'Why don't you call me "tu"? I'd rather you did.'

'Outside the camp I would have done, and I'd have asked you to do the same. Here, it's very important to talk to each other with the marks of respect that the kapos refuse us.'

'And with the organisers, do we use "tu" or "vous"?'

'You talk to them?'

PFX 150 looked annoyed. She took a moment to reply:

'No. But if an organiser or a kapo comes to ask me something, will I have to say "tu" or "vous"?'

'You say "vous" to everybody.'

Kapo Zdena came over to yell that they were here to work, not to chat.

That scrap of conversation haunted Pannonique. As she went on with her labour, she became aware that she had Schubert's *Erl-King* going around in her head. It wasn't the ideal music for the job. Normally, Pannonique programmed her brain to play symphonies that gave her the energy indispensable for such physical labour – Saint-Saëns, Dvořák – but now that heart-rending *Lied* stuck in her skull and sapped her strength.

Pannonique questioned the prisoners sleeping in the same hut as the girl. She didn't receive any meaningful reply. Most of them were so exhausted, so leaden with sleep, that they didn't hear the old woman's cries in the night.

'And yet she's housed closer to you than to us,' said Pannonique.

'I'm so exhausted that nothing could wake me up,' someone replied.

'PFX 150 is a good kid,' said someone else. 'She's well-behaved, and you never hear a peep out of her.'

In the evening, Pannonique made another attempt to talk to the child. It wasn't easy. She was as hard to hold on to as a piece of soap, and she took refuge in meaninglessness. Pannonique changed tack:

'What did you like in your life as a child?'

'I liked birds. They're pretty, they're free, they fly. I used to spend my time watching them. All my pocket money went on buying turtle-doves at the market, which I then freed. I loved that: I would take that warm, palpitating body in both my hands, release it into the sky and it would become master of the air. I tried to fly with them in my imagination.'

'Are there any birds in the camp?'

'Haven't you noticed? There aren't any. Birds aren't mad. It smells too bad here.'

'So you're really the bird of the camp,' Pannonique said affectionately.

PFX 150 immediately flew into a black fury.

'Just shut up about that!'

'Did I say something nasty?'

'Little bird here, little bird there, stop calling me that!'

'Do other people at the camp call you little bird?'

The child fell silent. Her lips trembled. She plunged her face into her hands. Pannonique couldn't get another sound from her.

The following night, she tried to stay awake. But sleep fell upon her as if concrete were being poured over her and she didn't hear a thing. She reproached herself: God wouldn't sleep like a log if he had someone to protect.

The next night, she had programmed her brain so thoroughly that she didn't close her eyes. She didn't hear anything, not even the old woman who, for incomprehensible reasons, abstained from howling at the moon.

That sleepless night filled her with a hateful weariness: God wouldn't feel anything like this. But still she didn't renounce her divinity: it isn't part of me and I take no pleasure in it; but it's too necessary.

ZHF 911 resumed the following night, wailing even more loudly than usual, and waking Pannonique, who got up like a sleepwalker and tiptoed outside. She ran to PFX 150's hut and hid. A very tall man, thin and strong, opened the door, holding in his arms a little body, gagging its mouth with his hand. He passed within the beam of the watchtower spotlight and Pannonique saw that he was very old and wearing a smart suit. He left with his booty.

She stayed crouching in the mud, her heart at breaking-point. It seemed to last for ever. When he came back, he no longer needed to gag the child: the little girl lay inertly against his body.

He entered the hut and came out alone. Pannonique followed him. She saw him going into the accommodation assigned to the people known as the 'officers': the chief organisers. She heard the door being double-locked.

Back on her mattress, Pannonique wept with disgust.

The next day, she studied the face of PFX 150: it gave no sign of anything at all.

'Who's the old man in the night?'

The little girl didn't reply.

Pannonique shook her furiously.

'Why are you protecting him?'

'I'm the one I'm protecting.'

'Have I threatened you?'

Kapo Marko came to yell at Pannonique:

'Have you stopped shaking that poor kid?'

As she cleared the rubble, she wondered, her fury at its height, if it was possible that the prisoners who slept in the little girl's hut had seen and heard nothing.

'I'm sure they're lying. They're dying of fear, the bastards. I'm going to intervene.'

She waited for Kapo Zdena to come over and told her that she wanted a meeting with an organiser. Zdena looked at her, as perplexed as if she had asked her for a roast turkey. But no arrangements seemed to have been made for such a case: off the kapo went.

One would have to assume that she passed on the message, because there was a reply: it was out of the question. Pannonique then demanded to know if she had any recourse. 'Where do you think you are?' came the answer.

Pannonique spent the day trying to find an arena within which she could reveal the scandal. By evening, she still hadn't found one. In the refectory, she was at the end of her tether. What if I got up, and took them all as witnesses, and cried out that I know? There would be no point. At best, there would be a mutiny, which would only end in a bloodbath. At worst, the prisoners wouldn't react, slumped over their awful food, and I don't want to risk being as disgusted with them as that. It's better if I intervene directly.

The following night was one of those in which the old

woman didn't howl at the moon. So Pannonique didn't wake up and couldn't protect PFX 150. The next morning, she was furious: to think that without that witch's bawling I slept without a care in the world!

The night after that, she was drawn from her sleep by the cries of ZHF 911. But by the time she reached the little girl's hut, the man was already long gone. She set off after him and, without thinking, hurled herself in his path.

He froze and watched her in silence.

'Let the girl go!' she ordered.

In his arms, PFX 150 shook her head at Pannonique, making strange signs, shaking her head.

'Let her go!' she repeated.

He stood stock still.

Pannonique went for his throat and she said:

'You're going to let her go, right?'

In a single movement, he hurled his assailant away like a projectile, then headed for the officers' accommodation. Pannonique grabbed his legs and brought him crashing down. The little girl rolled in the mud. Pannonique told her to flee, but her ankle was in the hand of her attacker, who got to his feet and set off, dragging her behind him.

Pannonique chased after him, yelling abuse:

'You piece of filth! It's easy for you, she's a prisoner. She's a kid, she has no way of defending herself. But I warn you, everyone will know. I'll tell the kapos, who will tell the organisers, I'll tell the viewers, I'm going to ruin your life!'

The man looked at her with an expression of hilarity, threw the child inside and then closed the door. Pannonique heard the sound of a key and then nothing. The silence was more worrying than a groan.

I don't even know that guy's voice. He didn't say anything, she thought.

She stayed prostrate in the mud and waited. In vain. The little girl didn't come out again.

At morning inspection, Pannonique saw Kapo Marko bringing the girl back. Pannonique smiled at her, and saw that the little girl looked like death warmed up.

Then Kapo Jan came to select the people condemned that day: normally he inspected the workforce and judged who should die; this time, without hesitation, he removed from the row ZHF 911 and PFX 150.

A tremor passed through the crowd. However accustomed one might have become to evil, the condemnation of a child was something else. They couldn't even rejoice at finally being shot of the old woman.

For the last time they heard the voice of ZHF 911, which still resounded half-way between a screech and a snigger.

'Opposites attract, you might say.'

She didn't care about dying.

PFX 150 was still stunned into silence. She had to be pushed to make her walk.

Pannonique had never suffered as much as she did seeing the little girl heading for her death.

It was clear that Kapo Jan had received orders. If I hadn't intervened, there wouldn't have been such urgency about getting rid of the victim, she thought with horror.

It was a terrible day: the child's ghost was in everyone's eyes.

Pannonique didn't allow herself to lapse into the paroxysm of disgust of which she was fully capable:

I've made a monumental mistake, it's true, but I'm not the

source of the evil. So here we are, I'm giving up being God, for the sole reason that it was a harmful idea.

At that moment, she saw frail MDA 802 stumbling beneath her heavy load of rubble. She ran over to help her friend carry the weight. Kapo Marko noticed this ploy and came over to push Pannonique away, shouting:

'Who do you think you are, St Simon of Cyrene?'

The girl trembled from her head to her toes. She could have gone on imagining that some kapos didn't even have the excuse of being brute beasts without a scrap of culture; what struck her was that without knowing it, the kapo had uttered the very words she needed.

Simon of Cyrene: why hadn't she thought of it before? He was the finest character in the Bible, because you didn't have to believe in God to find him miraculous. One human being helping another for the sole reason that his burden weighs too heavily on his shoulders.

Henceforth I shall have no greater ideal, Pannonique swore to herself.

Part Three

Zdena started slipping chocolate into CKZ 114's pocket again.

She had almost stopped beating her with the cudgel. It's much harder to beat a person whose name you know.

Pannonique had become even more beautiful since she had given her name. Her feat had enhanced her lustre. And besides, one is always more beautiful when designated by a term, when one has a word all to oneself. Language is less practical than it is aesthetic. If, seeking to speak of a rose, one had no word at one's disposal, if each time one had to say 'the thing that opens in the spring and smells nice', the thing in question would be much less beautiful. And when the word is a luxury word, namely a name, its task is the revelation of beauty.

In Pannonique's case, if her number merely designated her, her name bore her as much as she bore it. Were one to send those three syllables echoing down Cratylus' tube, the music would be her face.

There are people whose names just do not describe them. You meet a girl whose face cries out to be called Aurora: you discover that for twenty years her friends and relations have been calling her Bernadette. And yet such a blunder does not contradict this inflexible truth: it is always much finer to bear a name. Inhabiting syllables that form a whole is one of life's great concerns.

*

The kapos were annoyed by what they saw as tenderness.

'So tell us, Kapo Zdena – you've stopped beating her almost entirely since you've known her name!'

'Who?'

'Don't take the piss on top of everything!'

'Her? If I've been beating her less, it's because she's been more obedient lately.'

'Whatever. Discipline has never been taken into account. If you beat her less, we'll have to make up for you.'

'No, guys, listen, I had your agreement!'

'You promised us you would tell us something in return.'

'I have nothing to tell you.'

'Then find something. Otherwise we won't answer for what we'll do.'

Zdena immediately set about simulating violent blows on CKZ 114's back. But she could no longer hurl abuse at her.

Pannonique reflected that at the beginning the kapo gave her real blows and a fake name, and now she beat her with a fake cudgel and no longer yelled at her a name that had become impossible to shout because it was true.

To escape thoughts that finally led nowhere, CKZ 114 decided to turn to EPJ 327. Feeling loved by someone good was a powerful source of comfort.

He constantly sought her presence. He spoke to her at every opportunity. He understood that she loved the love in which he enfolded her. He was grateful to her for it: it had become his reason for living.

'I've had more of a desire to live since I've known you, which means, curiously, since I've been a prisoner.'

'You mightn't say that if you really knew me.'

'Why do you suppose that I don't really know you?'

'To know me really, you would have had to meet me under normal conditions. I was very different, before the raid.'

'In what way were you different?'

'I was free.'

'I could tell you that was perfectly obvious. I would rather say that you still are.'

'Today, I force myself to be free. It isn't the same thing.'

'That's true.'

'I was trivial, too, sometimes.'

'We all were. We were right. It's a nice talent, being able to take advantage of life's trivia. It still doesn't tell me what was so different about you before *Concentration*.'

'Heavens, I can't find the words. But you can believe me nonetheless.'

'I believe you. But the person next to me here is a real person, even if the circumstances are intolerable. So I can consider that I do really know you, perhaps better than if I'd met you in peacetime. What we are going through is a war. War reveals people's deeper nature.'

'I don't like that idea. It would suggest that we need to be put to the test. I think war reveals only one of our deeper natures. I would rather have shown you my deeper peacetime nature.'

'If by some miracle we survive this nightmare, will you show it to me?'

'If I still can, then yes.'

Zdena observed this rapprochement. She didn't like it one bit. What annoyed her most was the thought that he, who

65

was nothing, whom she could beat at will, send to his death if she felt like it, had the greatest power: which was to please – she didn't know to what extent – the girl who obsessed her.

Zdena was tempted to drag EPJ 327 over to the row of condemned prisoners: why not simply eliminate her rival? The thing that kept her from doing so was the realisation that he wasn't her rival: she wasn't in competition with him. It would probably be more intelligent to study the man's methods. Regretfully, she had noticed that he was one of those people who use words to charm.

And in that respect, Zdena felt she was in an inferior position. The only time in her life that she had thought herself eloquent had been in front of the *Concentration* cameras, when she had introduced herself to the audience: she had seen the result.

Like any failure, she despised those who excelled where she had failed. 'The smooth talkers' – that was what she called them – such a pain! How could Pannonique allow herself to be attracted by their waffle, the purring sounds they made? It didn't even cross her mind that a conversation might have a content. In her youth she had known people who chatted, she had listened to the vacuity of their alternating monologues – no one was going to do that to her. And besides, Pannonique had subjugated Zdena without so much as opening her mouth.

Her bad faith couldn't completely conceal from her the shock that she had felt when she first heard the girl's voice, and the impact of her words.

It's different, the kapo said to herself. She wasn't chatting. What's beautiful is when someone speaks in order to say something.

And suddenly she began to suspect: EPJ 327 was speaking to Pannonique in order to say something to her. That was

66

why she was captivated. The bastard had things to say!

She sought within herself for 'things to say'. In the light of Pannonique's shocking words, she had worked out the rule: a 'thing to say' was something in which nothing was superfluous, and in which information was exchanged which was so essential that the other person was marked by it for ever.

Zdena, dismayed, could find nothing within herself that corresponded to that description.

I'm empty, she thought.

Pannonique and EPJ 327 were not empty creatures, that much one could guess. The kapo suffered appalling pain at this discovery, this gulf that separated her from them. She took consolation from the thought that the other kapos, the organisers, the viewers and many of the prisoners were empty too. It was astonishing: there were many more empty people than full people. Why?

She didn't know, but she was gripped by one question: how could she learn how to stop being empty?

The prisoners were the only human beings who had never seen so much as a second of *Concentration*. It was their sole privilege.

'I wonder which sequences the audience is interested in,' said MDA 802 over dinner.

'I'm sure it's the execution scenes,' said a man.

'You'd fear as much,' agreed Pannonique.

'And the violence,' said a woman. 'The beatings, the screams, that must help them unwind.'

'Of course,' MDA 802 added. 'And the "emotional" sequences: they must make their mouths water.'

'Who,' asked EPJ 327, 'do you think are the most guilty?'

'The kapos,' replied the man.

'No: the organisers,' broke in someone who never spoke.

'The politicians who don't put an end to such a monstrosity,' said MDA 802.

'And what about you, Pannonique, what do you think?' asked EPJ 327.

There was a silence, as there was every time attention was drawn to the girl.

'I think the guiltiest ones are the viewers,' she replied.

'Aren't you being a little unfair?' asked the man. 'People come home after a hard day's work, they're exhausted, gloomy, drained.'

'There are other channels,' said Pannonique.

'You know very well that the television schedule is often the only thing people talk about. That's why everyone watches the same things: so as not to be left out, and to have something to share.'

'Well, let them all watch something else,' said the girl.

'That's what's needed, definitely.'

'You speak of it as though it's a utopian ideal,' Pannonique continued. 'It's only a matter of switching a television channel, it isn't even very difficult.'

'I don't agree,' declared MDA 802. 'The audience are wrong, sure. But that's a long way from saying that they're the guilty party! Their worthlessness is passive. The organisers and the politicians are a thousand times more criminal.'

'Their wickedness is permitted and therefore created by the viewers,' said Pannonique. 'The politicians are the emanation of the audience. As to the organisers, they are sharks who merely slip through gaps wherever they happen to be, wherever there's a lucrative market.'

'Don't you think the organisers create the market, just as an advertiser creates a need?'

'No. The final responsibility lies with those who agree to watch a spectacle that they could just as easily reject.'

'And what about the children?' said the woman. 'They get home from school before their parents, who can't necessarily afford a childminder for them. You can't check what they watch on television.'

'Just listen to you,' cried Pannonique, 'finding a thousand dispensations, a thousand indulgences, a thousand excuses and a thousand extenuating circumstances where you should just be simple and firm. During the last war, the people who opted to join the resistance knew it would be difficult, if not impossible. And yet they didn't hesitate, they didn't lose themselves in equivocations: they resisted for the sole reason that they had no way of doing anything else. And we might add that their children imitated them. You mustn't see those children as idiots. A child who has been strictly brought up is not the cretin some people try to claim.'

'Do you have a plan for society, Pannonique?' said the man ironically.

'Certainly not. I'm on the side of pride and respect, while they have room for nothing but contempt. That's all.'

'And what about you, EPJ 327, you haven't said anything yet, what do you think?'

'I'm horrified to note that there's only one person we can be sure would never have watched *Concentration*, and that's Pannonique. From that I conclude that she must be the one who's right.'

There was a general feeling of embarrassment.

'You would never have watched *Concentration* either,' said Pannonique to EPJ 327, when they were apart from the others.

'I haven't got a television.'

'That's an excellent reason. You haven't boasted about it. Why not?'

'You're the standard-bearer. I look a bit too much like what I am: a teacher.'

'That's nothing to be ashamed of.'

'No. But when it comes to galvanising people, you're the ideal. You talked about the resistance. Do you know that you could create a resistance structure inside the camp?'

'You think so?'

'I'm sure of it. I won't tell you how, because I don't know. And anyway, you're the tactical genius. That coup de théâtre with which you saved MDA 802's life, for instance, I'd never have come up with that.'

'I'm nothing like a genius.'

'That's not the issue. I'm counting on you.'

The rescue of MDA 802 had not been premeditated, she thought: strategies came to her in a second, inspired by the tension of the moment. The rest of the time, her thoughts were barely any different from those of the other prisoners: confusion, fear, hunger, exhaustion, disgust. She set about shrugging off all those ruminations and replacing them with music, the fourth movement of Saint-Saëns's Organ Symphony to give heart to her belly, the andante from Schubert's Tenth Symphony to give heart to her head.

The next day, at the morning inspection, Pannonique suddenly became convinced that she was being filmed: the camera was trained on her and wouldn't let her go, she could feel it, she was sure of it.

Part of her brain told her that this was nothing but infantile narcissism: when she was little she often had that sense that an eye – God? her conscience? – was following her. Growing up meant, among other things, the abandonment of belief in anything of the kind.

However, the heroic part of her being ordered her to believe it, and to take advantage of it very quickly. Without waiting a moment longer, the girl turned her face towards the imaginary camera and declaimed in a loud voice:

'Viewers, switch off your televisions! You are the guiltiest of all! If you didn't provide this monstrous programme with such a huge audience, it would have gone out of existence long ago! You are the true kapos! And when you watch us die, your eyes are our murderers! You are our prison, you are our torture!'

Then she fell silent, her eyes still blazing.

Kapo Jan had joined her now, and struck her as though to decapitate her.

Kapo Zdena, furious that he was encroaching on her territory, came to stop him and murmured in his ear:

'That's enough, the organisers are in on it.'

Kapo Jan looked at her in bafflement.

'That lot don't know what to come up with next,' she said as she walked away.

Zdena put the girl back in the row and whispered to her, staring into her eyes:

'Well done. I think the same as you.'

The day continued smoothly.

Pannonique was both galvanised and baffled by the fact that her gesture had gone unpunished. She said to herself that there was no harm in waiting. She couldn't rely on surprise for ever.

The prisoners looked at her with those appalled and admiring expressions reserved for crazed geniuses who condemn themselves to death with their insane behaviour. She read that appraisal in their eyes and grew ever more resolute in the choices she had made. And Zdena's approval of her invective was absurd in the extreme.

At dinner in the evening, Pannonique's unit were astonished that she was still alive.

'Can you tell us what came over you?' asked MDA 802.

'I remembered that phrase by an Algerian hero,' said Pannonique: '"If you speak, you die; if you don't speak you die. So speak and die."'

'Try and save yourself anyway,' said EPJ 327. 'We need you alive.'

'Do you disapprove of me?' she asked.

'I approve of you and I admire you. That doesn't mean I'm not afraid for you.'

'I can assure you that I've never been better. And that didn't keep Kapo Zdena from slipping the daily bar of chocolate into my pocket,' she said, distributing the squares.

'She probably hasn't received any instructions about what to do with you.'

'Did you know that she didn't wait for any, and came to congratulate me?'

And Pannonique prompted an outburst of hilarity by quoting the kapo's words: 'Well done. I think the same as you.'

'Kapo Zdena thinks!'

'And she thinks the same as our figurehead!'

'She's one of us!'

'We'd always suspected as much, from the way she yells at us and beats us.'

'She's a sensitive soul.'

'That said,' observed Pannonique, 'we owe her a huge debt: without her chocolate, some of us would already have died of hunger.'

'We know the reason for her generosity . . .' said EPJ 327 through gritted teeth.

Pannonique felt uneasy, as she did each time EPJ 327 allowed himself to comment on the passion that Zdena bestowed on her. He, who was nobility itself, lost the least trace of generosity of spirit when the subject of Zdena came up.

That night, Pannonique, still reeling from the impact of her outburst, slept fitfully. She started at the slightest sound and calmed down as best she could, firmly clasping her thin body.

73

Suddenly she woke up and saw, right next to her, Zdena, who was eyeing her hungrily. The kapo's reflex was to gag her mouth with her hand to stifle her cry. She beckoned to her to follow her on tiptoes.

When they were out of the hut in the fresh, cold air, Pannonique whispered:

'Do you often come and look at me like that, when I'm asleep?'

'That's the first time. I swear it's the truth. I have no reason to lie to you, I'm in a position of strength.'

'As if the strong don't lie!'

'I lie a lot. I just don't lie to you.'

'What do you want?'

'I want to tell you something.'

'And what do you want to tell me?'

'That I agree with you. The viewers are bastards.'

'You've told me that before. Is that why you woke me up?'

Pannonique was startled by the insolence of her own tone. It was stronger than she was.

'I wanted to talk to you. We never get the chance.'

'Perhaps because we have nothing to say to each other.'

'I've got things to tell you. You've opened my eyes.'

'What to?' Pannonique asked ironically.

'To you.'

'I don't want to be a topic of conversation,' said the girl, moving away.

The kapo caught her with an arm more muscular than her own.

'When I say you, I mean much more than you. Don't be afraid. I don't want to harm you.'

'You have to choose which side you're on, Kapo Zdena. If you aren't on mine, you mean me harm.'

'Don't call me Kapo Zdena. Just Zdena, plain and simple.'

74

'While you remain what you are, I will call you Kapo Zdena.'

'I can't change sides. I'm paid to be a kapo.'

'That's a rotten argument.'

'Perhaps I was wrong to agree to be a kapo. But now that I am, it's too late.'

'It's never too late to stop being a monster.'

'If I'm a monster, I won't stop being one by changing sides.'

'What's monstrous in you is the kapo, it isn't Zdena. Stop being a kapo, and you'll stop being a monster.'

'In concrete terms, what you suggest is impossible. There's a clause in the kapo contract: if we resign before the end of our year's work, we immediately become prisoners.'

Pannonique thought that perhaps she was lying.

Too bad she had no way of checking what Zdena said.

'How could you have signed a contract like that?'

'It was the first time anyone ever wanted anything from me.'

'And that was enough for you!'

'Yes.'

'A poor creature in every sense of the phrase,' Pannonique reflected.

'I'll go on bringing you chocolate. Hang on, I've kept the bread from my meal.'

She held out a little round, golden roll, very different from the horrible, stale bread given to the inmates. The girl looked at it and her mouth watered. Hunger won out over fear: she grabbed it and devoured it with gusto. The kapo watched her with satisfaction.

'What do you want now?'

'Freedom.'

'That isn't something you can slip into someone's pocket.'

'Do you think there's any chance of escaping?'

'Impossible. The security system is impregnable.'

'Even if you helped us?'

'What do you mean, us? You're the one I want to help.'

'Kapo Zdena, if you help only me, you won't stop being a monster.'

'Don't bore me with your morality.'

'Morality has its uses. It stops people making programmes like *Concentration*.'

'Doesn't work, then, does it?'

'It could work. The programme could stop.'

'You're crazy! It's the most successful programme in the history of television.'

'Is it?'

'Every morning we look at the previous day's viewing figures – it would make you faint.'

Pannonique fell into a desperate silence.

'You're right: the viewers are filth.'

'That doesn't excuse you, Kapo Zdena.'

'I'm not as monstrous as they are.'

'Prove it.'

'I don't watch *Concentration*.'

'You have a great sense of humour,' Pannonique spat with disgust.

'If I freed you at the risk of my life, would that be proof?'

'If you freed only me, it's far from certain.'

'You're asking the impossible of me.'

'If you're putting your life at risk, at least try to save everybody.'

'That's not the problem. I'm not interested in the others, that's all there is to it.'

'Is that a reason not to free them?'

'Of course it is. Because if I freed you, there would be a purpose to it.'

'What do you mean?'

'There would be a price. I'm not going to risk my life in exchange for nothing.'

'I don't understand,' said Pannonique, stiffening visibly.

'Yes, you do. You understand very well,' said Zdena, seeking her eyes.

Pannonique put her hand in front of her mouth as though to keep from throwing up.

This time the kapo didn't try to hold her back.

On her straw mattress, Pannonique wept with disgust.

Disgust at humanity for allowing a programme like *Concentration* to be so scandalously successful.

Disgust at humanity for including someone such as Zdena. And to think that she had seen her as a lost soul, a victim of the system! She was worse even than the system that had given birth to her.

Disgust at herself, finally, for awakening such desires in such a vulgar creature.

Pannonique wasn't used to this kind of disgust. That night, she suffered dreadful torments.

Kapo Zdena got back to her bed full of impressions that she could neither identify nor shake off.

She felt rather cheerful. She didn't know why. Perhaps because she'd had a long conversation with the girl who obsessed her. One which had gone rather badly, but that was predictable, and it would change.

Wasn't it perfectly normal for her to impose conditions on her liberation?

Deep inside her, there was a despair that dared not speak its name. In the watches of the night, it rose to the surface.

Sadness gradually made way for rancour: 'I'm the one setting the conditions, and too bad if madam doesn't like it. Power resides with the strong, a price is a price. If you want your freedom, you will submit.'

This resentment soon rose to a kind of ecstatic trance: 'If I disgust you, so much the better! I like displeasing you, and the price you will pay will only please me all the more.'

The next day, EPJ 327 saw that Pannonique had rings under her eyes. He didn't notice that the kapo had them too. He also noticed that the kapo was keeping her distance from Pannonique, and this brought him a certain relief.

But why did the prisoners' muse look so exhausted, so desperate? It wasn't like her. Until now, even on the hardest days, she had kept the strength of her eyes intact. Today, it was extinguished.

He had no chance to talk to her before evening.

Outside, the media went into complete convulsions. Most of the papers put Pannonique's coup on the front page: a big photograph of her addressing the audience. Some of them accompanied it only with her opening phrase in giant letters: VIEWERS, SWITCH OFF YOUR TELEVISIONS! Others, the second: YOU ARE THE GUILTIEST ONES! Some took as their headlines her most violent statement of all: YOUR EYES ARE THE MURDERERS!

Then her declaration was reproduced in full. Some leader writers dared to begin their articles with the words: 'I told you so . . .' Magazines asserted that it was a set-up, that the girl had been paid to say these things, and so on. Readers wrote in to ask if the prisoners were being paid to be killed as well.

Apart from these negligible interventions, everyone was unanimous: all the media agreed at great length with Pannonique, and glorified her. 'A heroine, a real heroine!' people cried rapturously.

*

At dinner, a confused Pannonique told her unit that she had had no chocolate that day.

'Of course,' said MDA 802. 'That's a reprisal for your invectives yesterday.'

'You see,' EPJ 327 continued, 'yesterday Zdena congratulated you for saying what you did, but she's the first to punish you for it. From now on we'll know what to think of her sincerity.'

'But . . . it's because of me that you have no chocolate this evening!' stammered the girl.

'You're joking,' protested MDA 802. 'The truth is that it's thanks to you that we've had chocolate for weeks.'

'Exactly,' said a man.

'If it hadn't been for my outburst yesterday, I could have given you chocolate today, too.'

'Given your heroism, we're happy to be deprived of chocolate this evening,' a woman proclaimed.

'And besides, that chocolate wasn't all that great. It wasn't my favourite brand,' said MDA 802.

The whole table exploded with laughter.

'Thank you, my friends,' murmured Pannonique, suddenly ashamed as she thought of the fresh bread she had devoured the previous day without a thought for her comrades.

Her remorse was such that she immediately gave her slice of stale bread to her people, who threw themselves on it without asking any further questions.

Two days later, the organisers were still marvelling at their viewing figures:

'It's extraordinary: never, never have we seen such an enormous audience!'

'You realise this: all the media applauded the girl's stand, and the result is precisely the opposite of what she was asking of the viewers.'

'As long as she goes on talking to them!'

'That kid really has a sense of showmanship!'

'She should be in television!'

General hilarity.

Kapo Zdena still didn't slip chocolate into Pannonique's pocket.

The audience of *Concentration* went on growing.

If she had known that her courage had led to this, it would have taken her to the depths of an already unbearable despair.

The journalists noticed the sad face of the muse. Many of the media spoke of the likely punishment that her declaration must have brought her: 'We should follow Pannonique's instructions all the more closely, because she has paid a high price for her heroism.'

The programme's audience figures kept on growing.

An editorial picked up this phenomenon: 'You're all despicable. The more indignant you become, the more you watch.' This foul paradox was repeated and drummed out by all the media.

The programme's audience figures scaled the heights.

A journalist in the evening papers repeated the morning's editorial: 'The more we talk about *Concentration*, the more we underline its atrocity, the better it works. The answer is silence.'

Amazingly, the media echoed this desire for silence. LET US BE QUIET! read the magazine headlines. The highest-selling daily paper filled its front page with a single word:

SILENCE! The radio stations repeated to anyone willing to listen that they would say nothing, nothing at all, on the subject.

The programme's viewing figures went through the roof.

'Still no chocolate?' a man at her table asked Pannonique one evening.

'Shut up!' MDA 802 commanded.

'Sorry,' replied the girl.

'It doesn't matter,' EPJ 327 said firmly.

Pannonique knew he was lying. He missed that chocolate terribly. You wouldn't have thought it to look at him, but for weeks those few daily squares had constituted their essential source of energy. And a pathetic crust of bread and a bowl of clear gruel weren't about to replace those precious calories. With each passing day, Pannonique felt herself weakening.

'You should harrangue the audience again,' EPJ 327 told the muse.

'Aren't you ashamed of yourself?' asked MDA 802.

'He might have a point,' Pannonique replied. 'I made my declaration to the audience two weeks ago, and you can see very clearly that apart from the disappearance of the chocolate, it led nowhere.'

'You know nothing about it,' said EPJ 327. 'We have no idea what's going on outside. Perhaps no one's watching the programme. Perhaps it's on the brink of cancellation.'

'Do you think so?' asked Pannonique with a smile.

'I think so,' said MDA 802. 'There's an Arab proverb that seems appropriate: "Don't give up: the miracle could be just around the corner."'

*

The next day, Pannonique murmured very quickly in Zdena'a ear: 'Tonight.'

The result wasn't long in coming. At about four o'clock in the afternoon, her overall pocket was stuffed with two bars of chocolate.

She spent the day in a state of terrible anxiety.

In the evening, at dinner, when she showed the chocolate, there were shrieks of joy.

'The sanction is lifted!' someone shouted.

'Come on, be quiet! Think about the other tables!' said the muse.

'And why don't you demand more chocolate?' protested the man who had complained before.

'Do you think I'm in a position to demand anything?' she said, feeling the anger rise in her.

'You could think before coming out with such nonsense,' said EPJ 327 to the man.

'If she's going to sell her charms, she might as well ask an exorbitant price, don't you think?' screeched the man who couldn't bear to be wrong.

Pannonique suddenly leapt to her feet.

'So how do you think I'm going to earn this chocolate?'

'Listen, that's your business.'

'Oh, no,' she said. 'If you eat it, it's your business too.'

'That's wrong, because I haven't asked you for anything.'

'You're worse than a pimp. To think that I'm risking my life to bring food to a creature like you!'

'I refuse to be a scapegoat. Everyone at this table is thinking the same thing.'

There was an outcry as everyone tried to dissociate themselves from such remarks.

'Don't believe them,' the man continued. 'They want to stay in your good books so that they can go on having chocolate. I'm merely saying out loud what they are think-ing. And there's one point that you're missing: it's that we don't care in the slightest how you earn that chocolate. All's fair in love and war, as they say.'

'Stop saying *we*, have the courage to say *I*,' broke in EPJ 327.

'You don't need to teach me any lessons; I'm the only one brave enough to say what everybody's thinking.'

'What strikes me as most amazing,' observed Pannonique, 'is how proud of yourself you seem.'

'One is always proud when one tells the truth,' announced the man, holding his head high.

Pannonique was granted one grace: she realised how ridiculous this individual was, and burst out laughing. It was contagious: the whole table began to laugh at his expense.

'Go on, laugh,' he squawked. 'I know what I'm saying. I've touched a nerve. And from now on I'm not going to have any chocolate.'

'Think again,' retorted Pannonique. 'You will go on receiving what you call your share.'

She waited until the others were sound asleep to leave the hut, and found herself face to face with Kapo Zdena, who was waiting for her.

'Shall we go to my room?'

'We'll stay here,' replied Pannonique.

'Like last time? That's awkward.'

It dawned on Pannonique that Zdena was suddenly imag-ining new possibilities that would benefit her no more than the old ones did. She took the initiative:

'I want to talk to you. I think there may be a misunder-standing between us.'

'Definitely. I wish only to help you. You just don't seem to know it.'

'That's another misunderstanding, Kapo Zdena.'

'I like it when you address me like that, even if I'd rather you left out my title. I like it when you say my name.'

Pannonique promised herself that she would not name her from now on.

The kapo came over to her. Pannonique was so frightened that she began to speak, her body trembling:

'The misunderstanding is this: you are mistaken about my contempt for you.'

'So you don't despise me?'

'You are wrong about the nature of my contempt.'

'A fat lot of good that does me. Explain.'

'What I despise in you,' said Pannonique, gripped by terror, 'is your use of force, of constraint, of blackmail, of violence. It's not the nature of your desire.'

'Ah. So you like this kind of desire?'

'What repels me about you is what isn't you. It's when you behave like a true kapo: it isn't you. I think you're a good person, except when you decide to be a kapo.'

'It's very complicated, all this stuff you come out with. Have you arranged to meet me in the middle of the night for you to spout this gobbledygook?'

'It isn't gobbledygook.'

'Do you hope to get off so lightly?'

'It's very important that you know you're a good person.'

'In the state I'm in, I couldn't care less.'

'The essential part of you yearns for my esteem. You would so love for my eyes to gleam with a fire for you that owed nothing to hatred, a reflection in which you were great rather than pathetic.'

'Even if I could see that in your eyes, it still wouldn't give me what I'm waiting for.'

'It would be better, infinitely better.'

'I'm not so sure.'

'What you seek can be obtained by force alone. And regardless of what you might think, you would be disgusted by it. When you thought about it later, it would be worse than a wave of nausea. You would be haunted by the memory of my eyes filled with intolerable hatred.'

'Stop. You're turning me on, you're filling me with desire.'

'If you really did have the desire you suggest, you would be capable of uttering my name.'

Zdena blanched.

'When one feels what you feel, one needs to say the other person's name. It wasn't by chance that you did everything you could to learn mine. And now that you have it, and have me before you, you are incapable of calling me by my name.'

'That's true.'

'And yet you'd like to, wouldn't you?'

'Yes.'

'It's a physical impossibility. We are wrong to despise the body: it's so much less bad than the soul. Your soul claims to want things that your body refuses. When your soul is as honest as your body, you will be able to say my name.'

'I assure you that my body would be capable of hurting you.'

'But it isn't your body that wants to do that.'

'How do you know these things?'

'I don't claim to know you. Contempt also means thinking you know the unknowable in others. I have an intuition about you, that's all. But your darkness is darkness for me, too.'

There was a silence.

'I am unhappy,' said Zdena. 'I didn't imagine this night

would be like this. Tell me what I can expect from you. Tell me what I can hope.'

For a quarter of a second, Pannonique found her touching.

'Could you say my name while looking me in the eye?'

'No more than that?'

'If you can, it will be tremendous.'

'I don't see life that way,' the kapo said, discomfited.

'Neither do I.'

They laughed. There was a moment of complicity: two twenty-year-old girls discovering, in consort, the world's ignominy.

'I'm going to bed,' said Pannonique.

'I won't be able to sleep.'

'As you lie tossing and turning, you will wonder what concrete assistance you can give to me and my people.'

Part Four

It came to pass that the audience ceased to grow. It didn't fall even slightly, but neither did it increase.

The organisers began to panic. *Concentration* had been in existence for six months, in the course of which the curve had been constantly rising, sometimes climbing very slowly, sometimes with peaks of growth for incidents publicised in the media – never stagnation.

'It's our first plateau,' said one of them.

'A plateau is only ever a false plateau,' said another. 'It's a law of nature: what doesn't advance retreats.'

'It doesn't stop our audience being vast, and still the most enormous ever achieved by any programme.'

'It's not enough. If we don't prepare for the future, sooner or later we're in for a nasty surprise.'

'Absolutely: the media have stopped talking about us. They spent months talking only about *Concentration* and now they've changed the subject. If we want to attract attention again, we'll have to find something.'

One of them suggested devoting a magazine to the main candidates, as had been done for the previous decade's television programmes, with photographs and interviews with the stars.

'Impossible,' came the reply. 'We could only imagine doing that with the kapos. And the real stars of the programme are the prisoners. And because we're reproducing the conditions of a real concentration camp, we can't interview them: it would be contrary to the principle of dehumanisation that governs any self-respecting camp.'

'So? Perhaps we should develop that idea. When CKZ 114 acquired an identity by revealing her name, we had amazing media coverage.'

'It only worked for her. And it's important not to make her discovery a commonplace.'

'The fact is that the girl's incredibly gorgeous. Shame she's calmed down a bit lately.'

'How's her love affair with Zdena going? That might be an idea, the torturor and the victim . . .'

'No, the audience like her being an unattainable virgin.'

'Anyway, that's not going to save us from the abyss. We need a new plan.'

The organisers worked away a while longer before gathering for a round-table meeting. They drank gallons of coffee and smoked.

'The only flaw in *Concentration* is that it's not interactive,' observed one of them.

'Interactive: that's all anybody's been talking about for twenty years.'

'And rightly so: the audience love participating. They love people asking their opinion.'

'How can we make our programme interactive?'

There was a silence.

'It's obvious!' exclaimed somebody. 'It's up to the audience to do the work of the kapos!'

'The cudgel?'

'No! Selection for execution.'

'I think we'll keep that idea.'

'Shall we broadcast a very expensive phone number?'

'Even better: do it with teletext. It's much better if the

viewer can sort everything with his remote control. He only has to type in the three letters and three digits of the number of the person he wants to eliminate.'

'Brilliant! It's like the games at the Colosseum in Rome, thumb up or down.'

'You're crazy. No one's going to participate. No viewer is going to designate his victims.'

All eyes converged on the man who had just spoken.

'How much do you want to bet?' asked someone else.

They all shrieked with laughter.

'The programme is saved,' decreed the head of the symposium, bringing the meeting to a close.

The new principles were explained to the audience so that they could be understood even by the most complete cretin. A smiling presenter announced enthusiastically that *Concentration* was to be *the audience's* programme.

'From now on it will be you at home who select the prisoners. You will choose who stays and who goes.'

The use of the word 'death' was carefully avoided.

A remote control appeared, filling the whole screen. The buttons needed to access *Concentration*'s teletext page were shown in red. It was very easy, but because the organisers suspected that some people wouldn't be able to manage it, they explained again: 'It would be a shame to lose your votes for a simple technical problem,' the presenter explained.

'We should point out that access to the *Concentration* teletext page is completely free, in line with the democratic principle of our programme,' he concluded gracefully.

The media screamed even louder than it had over the programme's birth: LATEST INVENTION OF *CONCENTRATION*: WE ARE THE KAPOS! read the headline on the main daily newspaper. WE ARE ALL EXECUTIONERS.

WHO DO THEY THINK WE ARE? said all the papers.

One leader writer was particularly impassioned: 'I appeal to the honour of humanity,' he wrote. 'Certainly, it has already plumbed new depths in making the most disgusting programme in history so successful. But in view of this wretchedness, I expect you, I expect us, to make the honourable gesture: no one should vote. I am calling for a boycott, if not of the show as such, than at least of participation in this act of infamy!'

The abstention rate in the first vote of *Concentration* was inversely proportional to that of the most recent elections to the European parliament: almost nil, which told the politicians that they ought perhaps to think, in future, of replacing the ballot-box with the television remote.

As to the audience of the first post-electoral broadcast of *Concentration*, it pulverised previous records.

Those are the figures.

On the first morning of the new version of *Concentration*, the prisoners were lined up in a row, as usual.

The kapos were so indignant at the new ruling which deprived them of their chief prerogative that only Kapo Lenka turned up to explain it to the deportees. When she had displayed her legs, perched on their stiletto heels, and reckoned that she had had the desired effect, she froze, thrust out her chest and said:

'From now on, the audience will vote to decree which of you will be withdrawn from the row. That's what we call democracy, I think, isn't that right?'

She smiled, took an envelope from her cleavage, opened it as though at the Oscar ceremonies, and read:

'Tonight's chosen prisoners are: GPU 246 and JMB 008.'

They were the oldest prisoners.

'The viewers don't like old people, as far as I can see,' added Lenka with a snigger.

Pannonique was completely stunned. Kapo Lenka's vulgarity added to her disbelief. It wasn't possible, it was too dreadful. Lenka had made the story up, she'd disguised her choice as a referendum. Yes, that was the only possibility.

What she found harder to explain was the attitude of the other kapos. They stayed grumpily in the background; Pannonique guessed at a quarrel between Lenka and her colleagues. But in the course of the day, the absence of the nymphomaniac kapo did nothing to alter their mood.

Zdena seemed particularly gloomy.

The next morning, there could be no more room for ambiguity. The prisoners stood in their line, Kapo Marko didn't even inspect them; he stood in front of them, took out a piece of paper and said:

'Since no one is asking our opinion any more, I won't act out the rigmarole of the inspection. Today, the soldiers condemned by the audience are AAF 167 and CJJ 214.'

These were two particularly shy girls.

'I shall take the liberty of finding this choice questionable,' proclaimed Kapo Marko. 'That's what happens when you ask the opinion of non-specialists. The opinion of the professionals was quite different, wasn't it? And in the end, *vox populi, vox Dei.*'

There was a veritable mobilisation of the media in the face of the ignominy represented by the massive participation on the viewers' part. By common accord, on the same day all the newspapers had headlines which read, in giant letters: ROCK BOTTOM! – and all began their single front-page article with: 'We've touched it.'

It was all the radio and television channels could talk about. The satirical magazines complained that words failed them: in terms of horror-comedy, reality had far outstripped them. 'The funniest thing about this wretched state of affairs must be the indignation of the kapos, henceforth deprived of their power of life and death over prisoners, and speaking gravely about the weaknesses of democracy,' one of them commented.

The result of this barrage was not slow in coming: every-body started watching *Concentration*. Even people who had no television went to their neighbours' houses to watch it, which didn't stop them boasting long and loud about being the last refuseniks, the last adversaries of the televisual rub-bish bin. It was all the more surprising, then, to hear them holding forth about this programme with full knowledge of the facts.

It was a pandemic.

Zdena was worried. While the kapos had decided upon the executions, she had had the power to protect Pannonique; now that the final verdict rested with the audience, she was no longer sure of anything. That was what she found most odious in the democracy whose existence she had just discovered: uncertainty.

She took reassurance where she could: Pannonique was the darling, the muse, the heroine, the beauty and so on. The viewers wouldn't be stupid enough to sacrifice their favourite.

The first vote dispelled her fears: if the consultation of the people led to the eviction of the oldest prisoners, then Pannonique was safe. The second vote revived her anxieties: two girls had been condemned just because they were rather withdrawn. Certainly, Pannonique didn't go unnoticed, but she was reserved – and she had been becoming more and more reserved of late.

In short, with such a ludicrous audience, you could suspect the worst. In the afternoon, as she slipped the ritual chocolate into her pocket, the kapo murmured: 'Tonight.' Pannonique assented.

At midnight, the two young women met up.

'You absolutely have to react,' said Zdena, using 'tu'. 'Why don't you speak any more? Why have you stopped speaking to the viewers?'

'You saw how useful my intervention was,' replied Pannonique.

'You won't change the audience, but at least you'll be spared! The two girls eliminated this morning were killed precisely because they were so insignificant. You must live. The world needs you.'

'And what about you, why don't you act? You don't take any trouble on our behalf. Two weeks ago, I asked you for a plan to save us. I'm still waiting.'

'You have more means at your disposal than I have. People are thrilled about you. Nobody's interested in me.'

'But look, you're free and I'm a prisoner! Have you thought of an escape plan?'

'I'm working on it.'

'Hurry up, or we'll all be dead!'

'I'd work better if you were nicer.'

'I can see where you're taking this.'

'You realise that you're asking the impossible of me, with nothing in exchange?'

'My survival, and my group's survival. Do you call that nothing?'

'How do I get it into your stupid head? I'm not asking all that much of you.'

'That's not how I see it.'

'You're a moron. You don't deserve to live.'

'In that case, rejoice. I'm not going to live,' said Pannonique, turning on her heels.

Until that moment, Zdena had been fascinated by the intelligence of the girl who obsessed her. Her way of speaking, saving up her words and answering when one least expected it, convinced her of the excellence of her brain. Now she had discovered that the girl was in fact too thick for words.

The idea of preferring death struck her as quite scandalous. Life was worth a bit of effort, wasn't it? And what she was asking for was as good as nothing at all.

Pannonique seemed to her to be behaving like one of those marchionesses in the novels she hadn't read, defending to the death grotesque virtues that they alone valued. Zdena dismissed that kind of literature with all the enthusiasm of someone unsure of its existence: generally speaking, the novelistic universe struck her as stupid enough to harbour such customs.

The worst thing is that it doesn't stop me loving her. It's as though I liked her even more. By balking so at the idea of giving me what is given so easily, by getting on her high horse as much as if I were demanding that she sacrifice her mother and father, she attracts me so powerfully that I could die.

A flush of joy filled the whole of her being as she felt such strong desire – checked by the memory of reality: Pannonique was going to die sooner or later. The most beautiful, the most pure, the most elevated and the most delectable thing that humanity had produced would be killed amidst terrible suffering before millions of viewers.

Zdena felt as if she were understanding the full horror of that information for the first time.

Then she decided on a plan that was a match for her passion. She would have to approach Pannonique's circle.

Her choice led her to MDA 802. She had hated the woman while she had seen her as a potential rival. Later, she had found out that she was mistaken: MDA 802 felt nothing but friendship for Pannonique who, oh misery, seemed not insensitive to the love of EPJ 327.

She surreptitiously slipped MDA 802 a phial of cochineal and whispered:

'Pretend you've got a bleeding wound, quickly!'

MDA 802's heart beat wildly: the kapo was trying to talk to her away from the others. Was she going to proposition her, as she had Pannonique? If that was so, she would leap at the chance. She felt no attraction for Zdena, but she was prepared to do anything to regain her freedom.

She spilled the cochineal into her palm, and then groaned, showing her hand.

'Blood's gushing out,' said Zdena. 'I'm taking her to the sick bay.'

She led her away, yelling at her the while:

'How idiotic you are, cutting yourself on the rubble!'

No one had time to react. Unnoticed by anyone, they went not to the sick bay, but to the kapo's room.

'We've got to talk,' Zdena began. 'You're good friends with CKZ 114, aren't you?'

'Yes.'

'Well, it's all one way. She's hiding things from both you and the unit.'

'That's her business.'

'Yeah, right. She's fully aware of the risk she's running.'

MDA 802 thought it better to remain silent.

'You don't want to grass on your mate, that's fine,' the kapo went on. 'She wouldn't hesitate for a moment.'

This is a trap, thought the prisoner.

'You know what I want from her. It's not such a big deal, is it? And if she let me have it, I'd guarantee that the whole unit would escape, including her, including you. But no: Miss Madam refuses, and by refusing herself, she refuses to save you.'

MDA 802's chest was puffed up with rage, an undifferentiated indignation directed as much at the kapo as at Pannonique. Pragmatically, she decided to defer her fury, and risk everything:

'Kapo Zdena, I won't refuse you what CKZ 114 refuses you.'

She was trembling convulsively.

Zdena stood open-mouthed, then laughed like an ogress.

'Do you fancy me, MDA 802?'

'A bit,' said the unfortunate woman.

'So you'll give yourself for nothing?'

'No.'

'Really?' laughed the kapo. 'And what's your price?'

'The same as CKZ 114,' she replied, on the brink of tears.

'Have you looked at yourself in a mirror lately? Lower your game, girl!'

'CKZ 114's life and mine,' the prisoner haggled valiantly.

'Are you joking?' bellowed Zdena.

'My life,' MDA 802 concluded.

'No, no, absolutely not!'

Then MDA 802 made a wretched suggestion that only those who consider themselves superior would allow themselves to judge:

'Some bread.'

Zdena froze with contempt and spat at her.

'You disgust me, you do! Even for free, I wouldn't touch you.'

And she threw her out.

'Go and tell the others what you know, now!'

MDA 802 was sobbing as she returned to the work on the tunnel. The prisoners put it down to the wound to her hand, which they thought had been disinfected. Pannonique, on the other hand, suspected something.

She caught MDA 802's eyes resting on her, eyes that were

humiliated and offended. She thought she read hate in them, too.

Pannonique shook her head in despair.

That evening, at dinner, it was plain that MDA 802 wasn't feeling at all well.

'Did Kapo Zdena hurt you?' they asked her.

'No,' she replied, staring fixedly at Pannonique, who didn't miss what was going on.

'Speak, tell us what you've got to say,' sighed the muse.

'Shouldn't you be the one to tell us?' asked MDA 802.

'No. You clearly need to speak.'

There was a silence.

'It's very awkward,' began MDA 802. 'Kapo Zdena told me she'd made suggestions to Pannonique, in exchange for which she offered us, all of us, the chance to escape.'

All eyes around the table turned to the muse, who remained blank-faced.

'Pannonique was right,' said EPJ 327.

'Do you think so?' asked MDA 802.

'She doesn't give a toss about us,' said the man who had never forgiven the mockery to which he had been subjected. 'She's condemning us to death by her refusal!'

'Shut up, you're a brute,' said a woman. 'Pannonique, I understand your misgivings. We all understand them. Kapo Zdena is a monster, and we'd all be revolted at the thought of agreeing to . . . to that. But it's a matter of life or death. Full stop.'

'You put a small price on honour,' said EPJ 327.

'Wouldn't it be an honourable act to save our lives?' protested the woman. 'You, EPJ 327, are madly in love with Pannonique: do you think we haven't noticed? You'd have to be madly in love to prefer our death and yours to an hour's submission to Kapo Zdena. We love and admire Pannonique, but not so much so as to sacrifice our survival to her hunger for purity.'

The woman fell silent. She had so fully expressed the general opinion that no one had anything to add.

'You're like the bourgeois characters in Maupassant's *Boule de Suif*,' protested EPJ 327.

'No,' said MDA 802. 'The proof is that I went and suggested myself in her place, and she refused me.'

Eyes lowered, the muse said nothing.

'Why are you silent?' MDA 802 asked her.

'Because I have nothing to say.'

'That's not true. We know that you're noble-minded. We'd like to understand you,' MDA 802 insisted.

Pannonique shook her head and sighed.

'Is it because it's a woman?' someone asked innocently.

'My reaction would be the same if Kapo Zdena were a man,' the muse cut in.

'We really need an explanation,' said MDA 802.

'You're not going to get one,' replied Pannonique.

'Princess on a pea, sending us to our deaths!' yelled the man.

He had shouted too loudly. The other units looked towards their table.

A long silence. When the atmosphere became less unbearable, the hubbub resumed.

'You're behaving like people defeated,' said Pannonique. 'None of you will be killed, precisely because I will have granted nothing to the enemy.'

The meal concluded gloomily.

*

The next morning, when the kapo had finished reading her envelope with the list of the day's condemned written on it, Pannonique took two steps forwards, turned to the place where she felt the main camera must be and declaimed:

'Viewers, vote for me tonight! So that when the votes are counted there will be not two names, but only one! Let number CKZ 114 be your totally unanimous choice. Numerous as you are, you have abased yourselves by watching this abject programme. Absolution will be granted you on one condition alone: that I am the prisoner condemned tomorrow. You owe me that!'

She stepped back and rejoined the line.

Alas, my fears are confirmed, she's round the bend, reckoned MDA 802.

And to think we were counting on her to save us! thought the rest of the unit.

Even EPJ 327 grew fearful: She's sublime. But you can be sublime and also mistaken.

Zdena was dismayed.

Pannonique spent the day in a state of complete serenity.

Press releases came pouring in one after the other, expressing the most recondite views.

One recurrent theme trumped all the others: 'She thinks she's Christ.'

In the evening, the same dispatch was sent out to all the media: 'Prisoner Pannonique spoke this morning to issue stern orders to the audience of *Concentration* to vote unanimously for her condemnation. She has unambiguously appointed herself as expiatory victim, declaring this to be the price of the viewers' absolution.'

The radio and television channels, less scrupulous than the newspapers, suggested that Pannonique had lost her mind.

The atmosphere around the table in the evening was awkward in the extreme.

'Is this supposed to be the Last Supper?' asked MDA 802.

Pannonique burst out laughing and took the bars of chocolate from her pocket.

'She took the chocolate, broke it and gave it to her disciples saying: "This is my body, which is given for you, take it in remembrance of me."'

'He wasn't so stingy with his body,' mocked the man who hated her.

'So I'm not him, and you're not Judas, who was a moving and indispensable character.'

'At least the other guy saved people!'

'You're rebuking me for not being Christ. That's pretty rich!'

'Even yesterday, you guaranteed that none of us would be killed!' protested the man.

'That's right.'

'How do you expect to do that? Are you going to protect us from beyond the grave?' he asked.

'Hold your horses a little. I'm not dead yet.'

'That thing you ordered the audience to do could well happen. You're quite persuasive, you know,' he said.

'I'm actually counting on it happening.'

'So when are you planning on saving us?' he snapped.

'Salvation is like two squares of chocolate: it's your due, isn't it?'

'Stop trying to be witty,' said the man. 'We're supposed to have smaller souls than yours. It doesn't mean that we wouldn't all have accepted Kapo Zdena's proposition to save the others.'

'You'd have accepted it for much less than that,' observed Pannonique.

MDA 802 started almost imperceptibly.

'Well, yes,' said the man who hadn't understood a thing. 'We're human beings, we're fully alive, we know that you've got to get your hands dirty from time to time.'

'Your hands?' Pannonique responded as though to something incongruous. 'Please stop telling me what you'd have done in my place. No one is in my place, no one's in anyone's place. When someone takes, on your behalf, a risk that would have been beyond you, don't claim to understand it, much less to judge it.'

'But that's exactly it, why take such a risk?' asked MDA 802. 'What Zdena was offering wasn't much of a risk.'

'It would mean losing for ever my conviction that in this

setting my desire alone is master. I have nothing to add,' concluded Pannonique.

EPJ 327, who had been frozen until that point, spoke:

'You know how right I think you are, Pannonique. But since your declaration, I've been frightened. I'm terribly frightened and, for the first time, I've stopped understanding you.'

'I'm just asking you, as one last favour, to talk about something else.'

'How could we talk about anything else?' said EPJ 327.

'In that case I demand the right to silence.'

Zdena and Pannonique met up at midnight, without even arranging to do so.

'You know what awaits you? You know how the execution works? You know what's going to happen to your frail little body?'

Pannonique blocked her ears and waited for Zdena's lips to stop moving.

'If I die tomorrow, it will be your doing. If I die tomorrow, you will be able to tell yourself every day that you condemned me to death, just because I wanted none of you.'

'Am I so undesirable?'

'You are neither more nor less desirable than anyone else.'

Zdena smiled as if she had received a compliment. The prisoner hastened to add:

'On the other hand, the method to which you have resorted makes you undesirable for ever in my eyes.'

'For ever?'

'For ever.'

'So what's the point in my saving you?'

'So that I will go on living,' said Pannonique, who was

amused by this kind of tautology.

'And what good will that do me?'

'I just told you: I will go on living.'

'That's no use to me.'

'On the contrary. The proof is that you're horrified by the idea of my death. You need me to live.'

'Why?'

'Because you love me.'

The kapo looked at her, startled, then she laughed, stifling her laughter so as not to be heard.

'You haven't the first idea!'

'Am I wrong?'

'I don't know. Do you love me?'

'No,' said Pannonique peremptorily.

'You've got a nerve.'

'You love me: it's neither your fault nor mine. I don't love you, it doesn't matter.'

'And I'm to save you for that?'

Pannonique sighed.

'We're not going to get out of this if you don't make your own contribution. You have the chance to redeem yourself, you're not going to pass it up . . .'

'You're wasting your time. Even if there is a hell, I don't care if I fry in it.'

'There is a hell, and we're in it.'

'Fine by me.'

'Do you think the conditions in which we met are ideal?'

'Without *Concentration* I'd never have known you.'

'Because of *Concentration* you never will.'

'In normal times, people like you don't meet people like me.'

'That's not true. I've always been willing to meet anyone at all.'

'So? You wouldn't have liked me.'

'I'd definitely have liked you more than I do.'

'Don't talk about me as though I disgust you.'

'Try reversing the situation: you can become the magnificent human being who will set the prisoners free and bring a repulsive experience to an end.'

'That won't win me your favours, as you say.'

'It'll win you my friendship and my admiration. You will love, and you will want more. I shall leave you now, I have nothing more to say to you. You need this night to come up with a plan.'

Pannonique walked away with a confident gait. She wouldn't be able to conceal her anxiety for much longer.

When she was alone once more, Zdena realised she no longer had any choice.

An escape plan was impossible to put into effect. She was a kapo, not one of the technicians who could have switched off the alarm.

She had to find some weapons.

She didn't sleep for a second.

Pannonique didn't sleep either.

I'm insane to take such a risk. That said, I was going to die anyway. I'm hastening my death, that's it. I shouldn't have done. I'm in no hurry to die.

She decided to remember the things she had liked in life. She ran through her favourite music, the delicate smell of pansies, the taste of black pepper, champagne, fresh bread, the finest moments with loved ones, the air after rain, her blue dress, the best books. It was fine, but it hadn't been enough.

The one thing I wanted to experience, I haven't!

And she thought, too, how much she had liked mornings.

That particular morning repelled her. It was as light as any morning. It was a traitor.

That fresh air was a traitor, too – what happened during the night for the air to be so new each morning? What was that perpetual redemption? And why were the people who breathed it not redeemed?

And that ineffable light, promising the perfect day, was a traitor as well, an introduction far superior to the day that followed.

'All the pleasure of the days lies in their mornings,' some-one once said.

Pannonique, on the last morning of her life, felt blurred.

As usual, the prisoners were grouped together on the esplanade for the announcement of those selected for death.

Part Five

It was live, the public knew – the word 'live' appeared in the corner of the screen.

Concentration won the total audience: one hundred per cent of the population. The programme was watched by everyone, literally. Blind people, deaf people, priests, nuns, anchorites, street poets, children, newlyweds, pets – even the rival channels had interrupted their schedules so that their presenters could watch.

The politicians sat in front of their sets, shaking their heads with despair, saying:

'It's terrible. We should have intervened.'

In the bars, people half-slumped on the counter delivered their diagnoses, eyes fixed on the screen:

'She's going to get it, is what I say. It's disgusting. Why did the politicians let it go ahead? They only had to forbid this kind of filth. The state has no morals, that's all I have to say.'

All right-thinking people thought the right thing out loud, their heads cocked sadly towards their sets:

'Such suffering! What a dark day for humankind! We haven't won the right not to watch: we must bear witness to such horror, we must bring them to book. When the moment comes, we will not say we were not there.'

In the prisons, the inmates watched and mocked:

'And they say we're the outlaws! We're the ones they lock up, not the organisers of this crap.'

But they watched all the same.

Innocent lovers, huddled cosily against one another, had

set up their televisions at the end of their beds.

'See how alien we are to this wretched world! Love protects us!'

The previous day, everyone had taken advantage of a moment's inattention by their partner to grab the remote control and tap in their vote.

The Carmelites watched in silence.

Parents made their children watch the programme to explain that what they were watching was pure evil.

In the hospitals, the patients watched, doubtless considering their pathology as an exemption of guilt.

The height of hypocrisy was reached by those without televisions, who invited themselves round to their neighbours' houses to watch *Concentration* and wax indignant:

'When I see that, I'm glad I haven't got a television!'

When they were summoned to the morning's roll-call, Pannonique noticed that Kapo Zdena wasn't there.

'She's abandoned me,' she thought. 'I have lost. I am lost.'

She sighed deeply. The air that filled her chest seemed to contain shards of glass.

Kapo Jan walked up to the row of prisoners, froze, opened the envelope and announced:

'Today's condemned prisoners are CKZ 114 and MDA 802.'

Once she had recovered from her astonishment, Pannonique took a step forward and declared: 'Viewers, you are pigs!'

She stopped for a moment to calm her beating heart. The cameras trained on her as she panted with fury. Her eyes had become a fountain of hatred. She went on:

'You do evil with complete impunity! And you're even

rotten at doing evil!'

She spat on the ground and continued:

'You think you're in a position of strength because you can see us and we can't see you. You're wrong: I can see you! Look into my eyes, you will see so much contempt in there that you will have proof of it: I see you! I see the ones who are watching us so stupidly, and I see those who think they're watching us intelligently, the ones who say, "I'm watching to see how low others will go" and who, as they do so, go even lower than everyone else! My eyes were in the television, watching you! You are going to see me die and know that I see you!'

MDA 802 was crying:

'Stop, Pannonique. You've made a mistake.'

Pannonique reflected that MDA 802 was going to die, and that it was her fault. She was ashamed, and fell silent.

In the room with the ninety-five screens, the organisers were watching the scene with delight.

'You'd have to admit that she's a star: there has never been a total audience, not even on 21 July 1969 in the United States. Why do you think she's the one to get it?'

'People see her as the symbol of good, or beauty, of purity, all that nonsense. They love the battle between good and evil. And the key to the show is purity executed by vice! Innocence tortured!'

'Quite simply, it's because she's beautiful. If she'd been ugly, nobody would have cared.'

'Nothing's changed since Paris and the golden apple,' said a literate piece of shit. 'Between Hera, Athena and Aphrodite, it's always the last who is chosen.'

*

The chosen one marched gravely towards her death, along with MDA 802 – the friend I didn't save, pined Pannonique, adding guilt to the rest of her suffering.

EPJ 327 called himself every name under the sun: You're going to let her die without trying to do anything, not even out of cowardice – what impotence! If only I could destroy the cameras that will show her death-throes! If only I could save her death, having failed to save her life! I love her, and it does no good!

He stepped forward and yelled:

'Viewers, feast your eyes! You have condemned to death the salt of the earth, and now you are about to see the death of the one person you would have liked to be, or the one person you would have liked to have! You need her annihilation because she is your opposite: she is as full as you are empty! If you hadn't been such nothings, you wouldn't have been unable to bear the existence of a person with substance! A programme like *Concentration* is the mirror of your life, and it's only out of pure narcissism that so many of you watch!'

EPJ 327 stopped when he noticed that no one was interested in him, and no one was listening.

Kapo Zdena had reappeared: she had led the two condemned women and their escort on to the esplanade. She placed on the ground some of the glass jars she had been carrying in her arms. She kept one in each hand and held them aloft.

'That's enough, now! I'm giving the orders here! In my hands I have enough Molotov cocktails to kill you all. I can destroy the whole camp! If anyone tries to shoot at me, I'll throw them and everyone goes up!'

She fell silent with obvious delight, aware that the cameras were trained on her. Several organisers came charging helter-skelter to the stage, carrying loudhailers.

'I was waiting for you,' she said, smiling.

'Come on, Zdena love, you're going to put them on the ground and come and talk to us,' said the paternalistic voice of one of the bosses.

'Now look here,' she yelled, 'my name is Kapo Zdena, and you call me *vous*, OK? I'll remind you that the Molotov goes off when the glass is broken!'

'What are your demands, Kapo Zdena?' the intimidated voice in the loudspeaker went on.

'I have no demands, I give the orders, I'm in charge! And I've decided that this crappy programme is coming to an end! All prisoners are to be released without exception!'

'Come on, you can't be serious.'

'It's so serious that I'm appealing to the rulers of this nation! And to the army.'

'The army?'

'Yes, the army! There is an army in this country, isn't there? Let the head of state send the army, and perhaps people will forget that he's been twiddling his thumbs while the inmates were dying.'

'How are we to know that those are real Molotov cocktails in your hands?'

'The smell!' she said with a broad smile.

She uncorked one of the jars. It stank of petrol and other even more noxious substances. The people put their hands to their noses. Zdena put the lid back on the jar and announced:

'I like this mixture of petrol, sulphuric acid and potassium, but it would seem that you don't share my tastes.'

'You're bluffing, Kapo Zdena! How could you have got hold of sulphuric acid?'

'There's as much as you need in an old truck battery. And there's no shortage of trucks at the camp.'

'A specialist is telling me in my ear that the basic liquid should be reddish-brown, not dark red like the one you're holding . . .'

'I'd be more than happy to allow him to test it, just to see him burn to a frazzle. It's pretty, isn't it, a Molotov cocktail? The liquids, so different, failing to mix . . And it need only come in contact with a potassium-soaked rag, and boom!'

Kapo Zdena knew her stuff. She was playing the role of her life, and she was jubilant.

Pannonique looked at her and smiled.

When the army circled the set of *Concentration*, the kapos opened the gates. The crews of all the television channels filmed the procession of thin, dazed prisoners as they filed out.

The Minister of Defence came in enthusiastically, and wanted to shake Kapo Zdena's hand. She refused to relinquish her glass jars, and announced that she demanded a written agreement.

'What, exactly?' asked the minister. 'A treaty?'

'Call it a contract, which will stipulate that you intervene whenever any television channel wants to make another programme like this.'

'Never again will there be such a programme!' protested the statesman.

'Yeah, sure. But you can never be too careful,' she replied, showing her Molotov cocktails.

The contract was immediately written up by one of the minister's secretaries. Kapo Zdena only put down one of the jars to sign the document, hold it up and show it to the camera.

'Viewers, you are witnesses to the existence of this contract.'

She gave the camera time to zoom in, and the public the time to read. Then she picked up the jars and walked towards Pannonique, who was waiting for her.

*

'You've been brilliant,' said Pannonique as they were leaving the camp behind them.

'Really?' asked Zdena, haughtily.

'There's no other word. Don't you want me to help you carry the jars? You might drop one of them, and it would be a shame if they went up now.'

'No danger of that. Apparently you can find sulphuric acid in old batteries, but I don't know how you get at it.'

'And the red liquid – what's that?'

'Wine. Haut-Médoc. It's all I could get hold of. I didn't soak the rags in potassium, but it is real petrol, for the smell.'

'A stroke of genius.'

'Does that change anything between you and me?'

'Until now, I've had an intuition about you. Now it's a certainty.'

'And in concrete terms, what are we left with?'

'It doesn't change anything about our agreements.'

'Nothing? You're tricking me. Under the guise of flattering me, you're actually pulling a fast one.'

'No. I'm keeping strictly to your premise.'

'What are you telling me?'

'You've been heroic. You're a heroine. Let the rest of your attitude be in keeping with that.'

'You're making fun of me.'

'Absolutely not. I hold you in the highest esteem, I couldn't bear for you to disappoint me.'

'You're trying to deceive me.'

'You're swapping roles. I've been honest with you from start to finish.'

'I've performed a miracle, and I confess that I hoped for just as much from you.'

'This is the miracle – any residue of contempt I felt for you is gone – you were, it must be said, the most wretched product of humanity, and now you are its most magnificent achievement.'

'Stop. What are you thinking of? I haven't turned into someone else, I'm still the person who was over the moon about becoming a kapo in that programme.'

'That's not true. You've been through a profound change.'

'No! All the things I did, I did to get you. I don't care a fig about being a good person. The only thing that counts for me is having you. Nothing in me has changed.'

'Do you regret being brilliant?'

'No. But I didn't expect it would all be for nothing.'

'That's heroism for you: all for nothing.'

Zdena walked on, staring at the ground.

They crossed various territories. It was an indeterminate Europe. They walked for a long time. Along the way, there was a small town.

'Let's go to the station. You'll take the train for your city.'

'I have no money.'

'I'll pay for it. I don't want to see you any more. It's a test for me. You won't understand.'

At the ticket desk, Zdena bought Pannonique a ticket. She walked her to the platform.

'You've saved our lives. You've saved humanity, what's left of humanity in this world.'

'That's OK; don't consider yourself under any sort of obligation.'

'Not at all. I have to tell you of my gratitude, my admiration for you. It's a need, Zdena. I need to tell you that meeting you was the most important encounter of my whole life.'

'Wait. What did you say?'

' . . . the most important encounter . . .'

'No. You called me by my first name.'

Pannonique smiled. She looked up at the girl and said, 'I will never forget you, Zdena.'

Zdena trembled from head to toe.

'And you still haven't named me, that's the other thing I wanted to say to you.'

Zdena took a deep breath, looked straight into the girl's eyes and said, as though throwing herself into the void:

'I am happy to know that you exist, Pannonique.'

Of what Zdena felt at that moment, Pannonique saw only the inexpressible wave that passed through her. She immediately boarded the departing train.

Dumbfounded, Zdena resumed her long march into who-knows-what. She couldn't stop thinking about what had happened.

Suddenly, she realised that she still hadn't put down her fake Molotov cocktails.

She sat down at the side of the road and contemplated one of the jars. 'This petrol and this wine, incapable of mixing, one floating above the other whatever happens, it reminds me of something. I don't want to know which of us was the petrol and which the wine.'

She put down the jar and thought she was going to explode with bitterness. 'You've given me nothing and I'm in pain! I saved you and you're letting me die of hunger! And I will be hungry till I die! And you think that's fair!'

Then she took the jars and hurled them against a tree, with all the energy of her indignation. The bottles shattered one after the other, the liquids didn't mix but Zdena saw that the petrol and the wine were absorbed by the same earth. She felt a kind of elation, and rejoiced like one inspired: 'You have given me the best thing of all! And what you have given to me, no one has ever given anyone before!'

Back at the Jardin des Plantes where this whole story had started, Pannonique spotted EPJ 327 sitting on a bench. He seemed to be waiting for her.

'How did you find me?'

'Palaeontology . . .'

She didn't know what to say.

'I needed you to know this: my name is Pietro Livi.'

'Pietro Livi,' she repeated, aware of the importance of this revelation.

'I misjudged Zdena. You were right. And yet you alone deserve the credit for what happened: you and you alone were capable of shaking her up.'

'What do you know about it?' She asked, slightly irritated.

'I know because I've been through it, and because I'm going through it still. My contempt for Zdena was wrong, all the more so because I am so similar to her. Like her, I think only of you.'

She sat down beside him on the bench. She felt suddenly happy that he was there.

'I need you too,' she said. 'Henceforth, a great gulf separates me from everyone else. They don't know, they don't understand. I wake up in the middle of the night, panting with anxiety. And sometimes I'm ashamed of surviving.'

'I could imagine I was listening to myself.'

'When the guilt becomes too strong, I think of Zdena and the miracle she accomplished for us. I tell myself I must prove myself worthy of her, to be a match for her guilt.'

Pietro Livi frowned.

'My life has changed profoundly since Zdena,' she went on.

'Have you stopped studying palaeontology?'

'No, you should finish what you've started. But now every time I meet a new person, I ask him his name, and I repeat that name out loud.

'I understand.'

'That's not all. I've decided to make people happy.'

'Ah,' said Pietro Livi, dismayed at the idea of seeing the sublime Pannonique devoting herself to charity. 'What does that involve? Being one of those ladies who go out and do good works?'

'No. I'm learning the cello.'

He laughed with relief.

'The cello! That's wonderful. And why the cello?'

'Because it's the instrument that most closely resembles the human voice.'